Bring Out the Wicked

A Collection of Short Stories

With thanks to Globe Soup
for bringing writers together.

Bring Out the Wicked

COPYRIGHT © 2023

Edited by James Hancock & Sarah Turner

All rights reserved. No reproduction without the prior permission of the authors.

FIRST EDITION

This book is a work of fiction. Names, characters, and incidents are products of the author's imagination, and any resemblance to actual events or persons, living or dead, is entirely coincidental.

Contents

Foreword   5

A Nice Place to Stay *very good*   7
By Sarah Turner

Final Trick *ok - nothing special*   17
By James Hancock

M.E.D.I.U.M. *ok - short nothing special*   23
By Ryan Fleming

Movie Night *ditto last one*   31
By Kerr Pelto

A Night Alone   39
By Christopher Bloodworth *short but good*

The Path of Totality   49
By Bryn Eliesse *didn't get it at all!*

Logs   55
By Séimí Mac Aindreasa *WTF?!*

Mercy and Death   63
By Jonathan Braunstein *Good*

Nobody Talks to the Grimm Reaper   75
By Mikayla Hill *Good albeit short*

The Rookery 81
By Sarah Turner

whatever!

The Neighborhood 87
By Kerr Pelto

ok - not much 'oomph' to it!

Stretched 97
By James Hancock

pointless & yuk!

A Family's Honor 105
By Christopher Bloodworth

same as last

The Lost Temple of Osiris 111
By Ryan Fleming

The Final Confession 115
By Jonathan Braunstein

Flesh and Blood 125
By Bryn Eliesse

Take the Plunge 131
By Séimí Mac Aindreasa

The Monster Within 135
By Mikayla Hill

Tricks, No Treats 141
By Kerr Pelto

All the Santas We Cannot See   145
By Christopher Bloodworth

Vortak: Evil Wizard   153
By James Hancock

The Architect   165
By Jonathan Braunstein

Human   171
By Sarah Turner

Proposal   177
By Séimí Mac Aindreasa

Reflection   183
By Mikayla Hill

The Tragedy of Montague Bellot   187
By Ryan Fleming

Ten of Swords   197
By Bryn Eliesse

Author Notes & Bios   205

Foreword

Every writer should know the importance of their beta readers and the invaluable feedback they bring. Other writers, especially those of similar ability, make the best kind of beta readers as they are fully aware of those little things which catch us out. Even the most polished stories have that out-of-place word, sentence, paragraph which escaped the author's meticulous edits. A typo here, a better way of wording something there; these highlighted areas are an essential part of the editing process. A story is only as good as the team who inspects it.

Much like The Avengers, every once in a while a team of writers assemble, and with a collection of stories, they create a thing. An anthology. A book. And then the editing process delves deeper, stories are tightened up, and the selection process begins.

The selection process for this anthology of short stories was *dark characters and/or situations*. Wicked moments, often created by wicked people. Not *horror* per se, but certainly leaning towards the grim. Not a book for kids.

And so the assembled writers brought forth potentially suitable stories; some were discarded, and others were given the nod. Three stories from each of the nine writers made the cut. Final edits were completed, and a book was formed. Short stories in the 500-2,000 word (with a little leniency) range.

Each of the writers herein has their own style, and as they come from different countries, their own slight variants of spelling. When editing, we looked for clarity, sentence structure and grammatical correctness above all else, and let the personal writing style and choice of spelling slide. The stories within these pages are the responsibility of the writer who created them. If a sentence is written in a certain way, it's because they wanted it said exactly like that. And who are we to argue?

We hope you enjoy the twisted tales within these pages, and if you find yourself recommending our book to friends, family, enemies, strangers in the street, we thank you.

A Nice Place to Stay

Sarah Turner

"You'll need a paper town," Mr Hudson said, hovering hawk-like over my desk.

I looked up, nonplussed.

"A fake place—a legal stamp to deter plagiarism." He chuckled. "Gee, for a cartographer, you sure look lost most of the time."

I was about to say that I knew what paper towns were, that I was merely caught off guard, when he spoke again.

"I'm heading out for lunch, so leave it on your desk when you're finished, and I'll glance over it." He plucked his hat from the many-tentacled stand, then turned back to me, dark eyes glinting. "Don't get lost now, Fred."

With that, he left the room, his formerly sharp frame spreading behind the frosted glass. I looked out the window to the icy street two floors below and saw him emerge, crisp again, under the sign for Hudson's Maps.

I had started here in summer when the fields were parched and yellow, and the green front door was peeling in the heat. It seemed there was always an opening for a new apprentice, so I took my chance. My mother had laughed, her fillings glimmering like loose change. "Maps? You've never *been* anywhere, Fred!"

The thing people don't realise about map-making is the trust it requires. It was true I had never left our county, but there was a trust that the places I'd heard of, and of which I held vague, jigsawed images in my mind, were out there in the world. I knew the depths and spans of oceans, the names of the roads that wrapped themselves about the country like grey ribbons, and I could recite the coordinates of cities—feel the dense weight of the nearest, just ten miles south, pressing at the window like fog. Without trust, the world was myth.

My map showed a sparse area two miles east of Greeswood and three miles southwest of Wolminster. I hesitated. Paper towns were common practice in some firms; I knew of a few up north, their phantom worlds bordering reality. But the part of me that put my trust in maps was wary. No matter, I would do what was asked of me.

I made a small mark, and from that mark, I added a B road, some cottages and terraced houses. Then a post office. A small school of grey stone. A church with a tall spire.

"Trinton," I said, smiling at my creation as I inked its name.

The road home twisted and wound through patchwork fields, but I could have driven it blindfolded were it not for the deer that sometimes bolted from nearby forests. Wooded areas were tricky to map, their sprawling forms resisting accurate depiction. They were counterpoints to towns, their dark masses hovering close by like shadows.

The car hummed, shaking me slightly as we drove towards the junction where a sandy-haired man sold flowers on Sundays. But instead of the junction, the road was headed towards a cluster of buildings and trees, dropping down into a village. The motor continued to burr; my hands trembled on the wheel. Where the hell was I? As if in answer, a large sign loomed into view in the dimming light, its metal feet planted in the grass. I stopped the car. There was a yellow acorn—the mark of our local council—in the top right corner, and running across the centre in large white letters were the words:

Welcome to Trinton
A Nice Place to Stay

It must have been some elaborate joke. The other workers breaking in the new employee. I reached for my OS map—a whole world folded in the glove compartment. Fulthorpe was there... Yes. Greeswood... Yes. Then... Trinton. I pressed my thumb onto it as if expecting fresh ink to plant itself into the grooves of my skin. But it didn't budge.

Outside, red kites were swooping low over the road; they'd been released some years ago as part of a reintroduction program and were now as common as gulls, only their bright underbellies marking them out as something special.

"It's like they're on fire," Mr Hudson had said as they soared past the window on the afternoon of my interview. He'd turned to me, his thick, silvery eyebrows knitted into a frown, his elbows resting on the large, mahogany desk between us.

"Do you know what we do here, Fred?"

I hesitated, sensing a trap. "Make maps, sir?"

Mr Hudson smiled.

"We create worlds." Behind him, rows of maps glittered in the afternoon sun, the cartographers' names etched into gold plaques underneath. Benjamin Wenlow, Matthew Sharple, Jack Wickes. Each name was different.

"This is my personal collection," he said, following my gaze. "Quite something, aren't they? I find a good map possesses a certain power—an ability to draw you in."

I'd never heard of several of the places. Clearly, I had a lot to learn.

Determined not to make a fool of myself, I put the map away, stepped out of the car and walked past the sign.

I had been to villages like this as a boy, had juddered over their cobbles on my bicycle and bought fat sticks of fudge from shops smelling of stale sponge and damp stone. They were two a penny in this part of the country.

To my right was a smattering of cottages with faded B&B signs tacked to small windows. I pushed my face to the glass of one, but the netting was so thick I couldn't see anything past the cloth flowers on the sill, petals pale from too much sunlight. I knocked on the door: no answer. They had an air of neglect; the paint on the windowpanes cracked and peeling. An abandoned village, perhaps? I knew they existed—whole communities upping and leaving, their homes hollow and forgotten. But there had never been any record of one round here.

Past the cottages, the road twisted slightly so that the whole village came into view. There was a post office to my left, its red sign clattering in the breeze, and opposite, was a small stone school with crudely cut bunting hanging from wrought iron railings. Beyond that, the road rose up to the vague outline of white terraces and the point of a spire, so sharp you could prick your finger on it. All quiet, all seemingly uninhabited.

I was about to wander back to the car when the streetlamps switched on. I blinked. The poles were bowed at the top like old men, and light slipped through their aging fingers, spreading across the pavement, climbing stone walls. Up by the church, someone was moving, stepping out onto the cobbled road. They were too distant to discern much, but it was definitely a person. Perhaps the vicar.

I cupped my hands around my mouth and shouted, "Hello!"

The figure stopped abruptly. They were tall and slim, with the outline of a hat on their head. I couldn't make out the face, but I knew it was turned towards me.

"Excuse me!" I called again, waving my hand.

The figure didn't move, just stood, feet planted wide. I dropped my hand. There was something unfriendly about it all, them standing in the middle of the road like that. Whatever were they playing at?

Back to the car, I thought. I'd had enough of this place. I turned and started walking up the sloping road, past the line of drab cottages. But as I reached the one with flowers in its window, I stopped. Something had moved behind the thick nets. A trick of the light, perhaps. I hesitated for a moment, feeling the heavy silence of the whole town, then carried on.

I half expected someone to have done away with my car, but it was exactly where I'd left it, the fields a pale grey behind, the moon a faint fingerprint pushed into an inky sky. It would take an extra half hour to get back via the long road, but at least I'd be home and out of this strange place. I thought about what I'd do—have a bowl of soup, perhaps, and listen to the radio. There was often something decent on in the evenings. I tried to picture my small living room and myself sat curled in the armchair, but I found I couldn't remember the colour of the walls or the shape of the chair or the particular pattern of the carpet that lay beneath my feet. It was all a murky darkness.

The road rose as it snaked away from the village until only fields and the black mounds of forests were in view. In a few minutes, I'd turn onto King's Street with its beamed pub on the corner, windows bright like jewels, jukebox whirring. Sometimes on a Friday night, I'd sit in one of the booths with others from Hudson's and we'd drink cider from cloudy glasses and choke on fat cigars. But what was that coming up on the left? It looked like the sandy-haired man who sold flowers! He must have been hoping to drum up extra business. With relief, I pulled up and rolled down the window.

"What'll it be then, sir?"

In the evening light, his hair was more grey than sandy, and his face was different to the one I had pieced together from blurry drive-bys.

"Oh god, I'm so pleased you're here. Do you know what's happening?"

"Chrysanthemums? All out of chrysanthemums, I'm afraid."

"No, listen. I'm trying to get home, but I appear to be lost. Something's happened to the road."

"Roses?" He smiled. "If it's for a lady in your life, I'd recommend roses." He pointed behind him to several bunches, indistinguishable in the twilight. "Red? Pink? Yellow?"

I was getting angry.

"Please! I need an explanation!"

"Carnations are best for funerals. Are you going to a funeral, sir?"

I brought my foot down hard on the pedal and left the man smiling stupidly at the roadside. It occurred to me to look in my mirror, to see him small and receding, but I couldn't bring myself to do it. One thing was for certain, though—I wouldn't stop for him again.

I prepared to turn onto King's Street but must have missed the exit in all the confusion. On the horizon, something was emerging. A thin tower. No—a church spire. I slowed to a crawl and hunched over in my seat so I could look up.

The church gave no signs of life save for an illuminated clock on the main tower, its moon-like face showing almost six. That seemed right. There were panels of stained glass shimmering faintly, and on them, I could just make out figures—hands clasped, wide eyes on something far above.

On the other side of the cobbled road, white terraces appeared, ghostly and looming, long cracks splitting their paintwork. The school was up ahead. The post office. The cottages with small, netted windows and empty rooms. Trinton.

Something rose in my throat, tight and clawing. I would drive. I would drive until it was light again. Never stopping, never letting anyone or anything get near. Yes, I would just drive! I pushed down hard on the pedal: the motor sputtered and growled. No, there was enough petrol. I pushed down again: it gave a feeble cough. A third time: nothing.

The church bell began to issue a dull peal, marking the hour. My hand was on the door handle, but something was happening outside. Lights were coming on in all the houses—even the post office and the school. Hunched shadows were moving past windows, shifting behind curtains. Above, red kites scattered, their bellies flashing danger. The bell chimed six and the doors opened.

A tall, hatted figure emerged from the nearest house and walked slowly towards me. It must have been the man I saw earlier by the church—but wait! Relief swept through me.

"Oh, thank goodness! I thought... What's going on?"

Other figures were stepping out of their porches now, their faces rendered silhouettes in the orange light.

"I've been trying to leave, but..."

Sharp eyes flashed beneath silver brows.

"Leave? My dear boy, why would you ever want to leave Trinton?"

'Apprentice needed. Enquire within.' Mr Hudson turned the dial on the typewriter and removed the sheet of paper. He'd get one of the lads to tack it to the door later. There was no rush. He glanced across his desk to where the map lay, framed in gold, its glass sheet shining yellow in the morning light. This one was a beauty; it deserved a spot on the wall. Fred's plaque would be ready to join it in a few days. He stood up and hung it next to the others, smiling at the little inscription:

Trinton
A Nice Place to Stay

Final Trick

James Hancock

Trick. *Slang. Prostitution term, meaning 'client' or 'the act of sex'. To turn a trick: Engage in sex for money.*

Mindy was understandably on edge. She chewed the skin around her stubby fingernails and fought to take her mind elsewhere. But it was no use; the cause for worry was right in front of her. Through the storm and hidden away in a seedy room. After years of seedy rooms, Mindy knew what to expect before she'd stepped inside. But you never know 'exactly' who you're going to get.

Angel leaned in close, moved a golden lock aside, and gently kissed Mindy's cheek. A swollen cheek, thick with blusher, concealing the yellow of fading bruises.

"One more trick, and then we're out. Okay?" Angel whispered into Mindy's ear.

Her attention fixed on the motel, Mindy nodded and tried for a smile.

Angel checked herself in the rear-view mirror, opened the car door, and climbed out. "I won't be long."

She pulled her coat collar around her neck, slammed her car door shut, and moved with haste as the rain hammered down. Twenty awkward paces in high heel shoes, and she stood in cover by the door of motel room six. She waited, watching Mindy shift seats to the driver's side; and then a faint orange glow as a cigarette was lit.

The rain thrashed and bounced against a blue pickup truck parked nearby. The only two vehicles in sight. A cold and miserable night on the dismal edge of a forgettable town. The shitty end of nowhere, with more of the same as far as the road takes you. Somewhere there was sunshine. Beyond the map of familiarity. But not here.

The motel walls were piss yellow, with a dozen faded red doors in a line and chocolate brown curtains closed across every window. Curtains don't shut out the darkness, but they hide it well enough.

Angel knocked on the door and waited.

"Yeah?" came a gravelly deep Southern accent. "Who's that?"

Angel brought her mouth close to the door. "Angel."

The door opened. You don't judge a book by its cover, but if the pickup truck was the cover, this book fitted it perfectly. Cowboy boots, jeans, denim shirt, and hat to match. The outfit wrapped perfectly around the gift inside it, and the gift was called Bret. God's gift, if you asked him. He looked Angel up and down, nodding his approval.

"Damn!" was all he could muster.

Angel was half Korean, half American, and all beauty. Stunning. If she was an actress or singer, her face would decorate teenage boys' walls all over the US. But she wasn't. She was a hooker.

"Full of eastern promise." Bret had moved on to sentences.

Angel didn't wait for an invitation and walked through the doorway and into the motel room. Bret shut the door behind her. And locked it.

Double bed, bedside table with phone, wall TV above a chest of drawers, and another door leading to the bathroom. Everything in shades of brown and cream. Basic, practical and without personality. Like so many rooms before it, Angel's office was impressively unremarkable.

"You wanna beer?" Bret moved over to a bottle he'd already started.

"No thanks," she replied.

He swigged his beer and stared at her. There was an uncomfortable silence.

"I can do what I want, right?" He looked serious, as if unsure of something. "Five hundred and I get to do whatever I want."

He reached into his jeans pocket and pulled out a folded bundle of twenties.

"Within reason," Angel replied, looking at the rings on his fingers and a line of five beer bottles on the chest of drawers. She knew the type. Liked to be in charge, yet often lost control of themselves in the heat of the moment. Bottles, knives, fists with big solid rings; she'd seen some of the other girls after a night with a wild mustang. Not her.

Bret held the money out, then pulled it away from Angel as if teasing her. She didn't bite. Some girls were desperate, but she wasn't.

"Hold on now. I've hired the room all night, and I wanna get my money's worth. Okay?"

"You won't be disappointed," Angel said, staring him in the eyes. He grinned and placed the money on the bed.

"Good. 'Cos I ain't payin' if you ain't playin'." He took off his hat and dropped it beside the money.

"I'm going to freshen up." She walked past him, towards the bathroom. "Make yourself comfortable. I won't be long."

"Hell yeah!" Showing his excitement, Bret slapped Angel's ass as she passed him. Too hard. She didn't let it show, but that was a warning right there.

She stepped into the bathroom and shut the door.

Bret unbuttoned and removed his shirt with impressive speed, displaying muscles, tattoos, and several bar fight scars. He leaned over the bed and lifted up a dirty old duffle bag. Throwing the bag onto the bed, he unzipped it. Out came his toys: a coil of rope, handcuffs, blindfold, pocketknife, bottle of bourbon, and a Zippo lighter. He flicked open and lit the Zippo, running his hand over the flame to test his pain threshold, then snapped it shut. He pulled his jeans' belt free in one fluid whiplike motion and wrapped it around the knuckles of his left hand. The leather creaked as Bret squeezed a tight fist.

"Come on, girl!" Bret was getting himself fired up. He was ready. "Let's get the party started!"

The bathroom door opened. Angel stood facing Bret with a revolver aimed straight at him. Bret's pumped up excitement deflated, and his grin dropped. He was expecting sexy lingerie, but Angel had done nothing more than remove her snubnose special from concealment, check it one last time, and get ready for business.

"What the hell's that!" Bret's tone had gone from cocky to nervous. "Hey! Don't point that at me!"

Angel glanced at the bed. "I thought we were bringing toys to the party. Was I mistaken?"

Bret took the belt off his hand and threw it on the bed.

"You used a similar selection of toys last week, if you recall?" She took a step closer to him. "On my friend, Mindy."

Bret shook his head in denial, held up his hands, and was about to blurt a pathetic lie, but Angel wasn't done... "On her face." Angel lowered the pistol to point at Bret's groin. "Nine stitches and a broken jaw."

"Now hold on there! I paid her well. She knew what I was buyin'..." Bret had more to say, but his defence was cut short by a flash and thunderous crack from the pistol. He buckled and collapsed, grabbing his bloody wound and squealing in pain.

Angel scooped up the money and knife from the bed. Bret twisted in agony, crying and mumbling unrecognisable pleas. A headless snake writhing at her feet.

Affording herself a final moment with her prey, Angel crouched beside him.

"She wasn't for sale."

Bret was a twitching mess of cold sweat and hot blood; his hands locked around his groin, attempting to slow the flow and ease the pain. He was failing on both counts.

"There's a hospital twenty miles down the road." Angel stood up. "If you're quick, you might just make it." She stepped over him, unlocked the door, and left the room.

Out in the rain, she calmly yet purposefully walked to Bret's pickup, opened the pocketknife, and stabbed it into the driver's side tyre. Tearing it free, a satisfying hiss followed as she repeated the act on the rear tyre before walking back to her own car.

Helpless and alone, Bret's fading screams were lost in the storm.

Five hundred would ease Mindy's pain, but defusing Bret was the objective. One final trick.

"It's done," Angel said, and gently kissed the scratch on Mindy's lip. "New town. Fresh start."

Mindy smiled and started the engine.

Task complete, the car pulled away and drove into the night. To better things. Off the map and towards the sunshine beyond.

M.E.D.I.U.M.

Ryan Fleming

Once again, Sophie found herself in a small consultation room, only this time, she was alone. About a year ago, she and her mother sat down with Dr. Wells, her father's attending physician. The brief conversation that ensued had concluded a seventy-one-day fight for Sophie's father's life.

As the two women said their tearful goodbyes before removing Sophie's father from life support, the question Sophie had been asking for the last two months was no less resolved: "Are we doing the right thing?"

Now that it was her mother in the intensive care unit, the question had birthed a new thought, a new terror – what if her father suffered? Was it right to keep someone alive like *this?*

In the cramped room, Sophie sipped from her Styrofoam cup, her fourth stale coffee of the morning. Her mind warred with the hope Dr. Wells provided, and yet, being here again triggered painful memories of her mother standing over her unconscious father.

Fragments of conversations from that hospital room bombarded Sophie's mind:

"Is he in pain?"

"I think the machine is doing all the breathing for him."

"Do you think he can hear us?"

"Even with his eyes closed, he looks so tired."

And then, of course, there was her mother's final question: "Does he want all of this treatment?"

How could they know? Even with Dr. Wells' knowledge and guidance, they had felt plagued with guilt and indecision over the choice to prolong her father's deterioration. The idea of making those decisions again—alone—was suffocating. The wall clock mocked Sophie, reminding her she passed each minute in uncertainty.

But what if she *could* know? The weight of that question had driven her to this room.

Sophie jumped when the door to the consultation room opened. A dark-haired man wearing thin-rimmed glasses and a lab coat entered, clipboard in hand. "Sophie Verne?" said the man in a distinctively German accent.

Sophie nodded.

"I am Dr. Gernsbeck," he said. He shook Sophie's hand and took a seat. "Your mother's attending physician, Dr. Wells, tells me you requested my services."

Fighting back the tears, Sophie said, "Yes, but I don't think he approves of me from speaking with you. He thinks there is a chance Mom will get better, but there will be a long and exhausting journey ahead." Sophie drew in a deep breath and summoned what courage she had left. "I was told you can communicate with unconscious patients." The statement seemed so ridiculous as the words left her lips.

Dr. Gernsbeck gave a gentle smile. "Me? No. But my machines, yes. They can successfully create a virtual reality for you and your mother to communicate within. I call it M.E.D.I.U.M., Mind Expression During Image Upload and Manipulation."

"Will it let me talk with my mom – ask her if she wants..." Sophie swallowed and continued. "...to be treated like my father?"

"You will be able to converse with a projection of your mother, yes."

Sophie's chin quivered as she dared to hope the words were true. She could *actually* ask her mother what she wanted, and the decision wouldn't rest on her shoulders alone.

"Does the process hurt?"

"No, no. It has no effect on the patient. It will conduct a neural scan to map out which memories will be best to transmit from. M.E.D.I.U.M will then tap into the temporal lobes to access your mother's memory, and the program will construct a virtual setting familiar to you both. Next, I will use low doses of electrical impulses to stimulate the sections of the frontal lobes to ensure speech, reasoning, judgment, and emotions are intact and that they can be translated via M.E.D.I.U.M. to the constructed virtual plane."

Sophie could only nod at the explanation, holding back what few tears remained.

Dr. Gernsbeck produced a sheet of paper. "I need your consent. This is still new technology, and I cannot always guarantee the outcome."

"Is it safe?"

"It won't hurt the patient, Miss Verne. I will see what you will see, but I cannot promise it will be a pleasant experience for you. The brain is a powerful organ, and we are only beginning to understand it through M.E.D.I.U.M.'s virtual reality."

After Sophie signed the document, Dr. Gernsbeck left and was replaced by a technician with a laptop wired to a metallic cap with electrodes jutting out from its interior. Once the electrodes were placed on Sophie's face and scalp, the technician tapped on his keyboard.

"To get a precise neural mapping of your brain, you will need to relax. Close your eyes, Miss Verne, and think of happy memories."

Sophie did as she was instructed, but her mind wandered to her questions.

After a few moments, the device gave a chime of completion, and the technician began packing up his equipment.

"Your neural mapping is complete. Please wait here while I scan your mother. The program will construct a virtual rendezvous so your brain can link to it. Dr. Gernsbeck has already informed Dr. Wells and the intensive care team of our procedure, so they will not interfere."

With renewed anticipation, Sophie watched the hands on the clock for an hour before Dr. Gernsbeck returned. "All is prepared, Miss Verne."

Sophie entered her mother's room and was overcome with the sounds of the ventilator breaths and beeps from the heart monitor. She stepped around the continuous dialysis machine and the various tubes emerging from her mother's chest and abdomen. Sophie sat in a chair next to the hospital bed. She reached for her mother's hand and whispered, "See you in a second." A chrome cap already concealed her mother's face. Wires from the helmet ran the length of the bed and into Dr. Gernbeck's laptop.

Dr. Gernsbeck slid a chrome headset over Sophie's face and eyes. All sounds faded as she stared into the darkness.

Through the speaker inside Sophie's headset, Dr. Gernsbeck spoke. "The initial feeling of disorientation is normal and will pass."

Sophie nodded, and Dr. Gernsbeck counted down to initiate M.E.D.I.U.M.'s virtual reality program.

The world around Sophie flashed white, momentarily blinding her. She blinked rapidly, and her eyes slowly adjusted to the images before her. As her surroundings came into focus, she found herself sitting on a stool in her childhood kitchen. Sounds of the washing machine and oven timer could be heard in the distance. Sophie saw her mother's back as she stirred a pot of bubbling stew.

"Mom?" said Sophie.

Sophie's mother pivoted like a rag doll. Her weathered face drooped, and her eyes were blankly transfixed on the kitchen counter in front of Sophie.

"Sophie?" mumbled the image of her mother.

"Yes, Mom! I'm here!" Sophie reached out and bumped the hospital bed of the real world with her hand.

"Why am I here?" said the image, wincing.

"A brilliant doctor found a way for us to communicate. You're…very sick."

The unblinking eyes of Sophie's mother crept across the room until they locked onto Sophie. "No."

"Yes, just like Dad."

"No!" shrieked the image of Sophie's mother.

Sophie jumped in her chair.

The image's face contorted and snarled. "No, I am here because you won't let me go."

Sophie could feel the tears forming. "But don't you want to be treated?"

Sophie's mother's face tightened into a gritted smile. "Treated? Can you not see I'm in agony?"

"The doctors and nurses assured me that..."

The image of Sophie's mother let out a wailing cry. "You saw what torment your father went through – artificial life with tubes, drains, and machines. Now, I suffer as he did."

"I just wanted to know if..."

The image grabbed its distorted face and let out a horrifying screech. "So much pain! Why won't you let me die!? Do you not love me?"

Sophie flung off the headset and hyperventilated. Her eyes barely had time to focus on her mother lying in bed when the uncontrollable howling began. Sophie clutched her mother's hand. "I'm so sorry."

A nurse entered the room, and Dr. Gernsbeck intercepted her before she reached Sophie. "It's okay, Miss Verne. I am still here with you."

"She wants...us...me...to...," babbled Sophie. Seeing the nurse behind Dr. Gernsbeck, she continued. "She is in pain. Oh God, she is in so much pain! Why am I doing this to her?"

"Doing what to her, Miss Verne? We are giving her the best possible care," said the nurse.

"No!" shouted Sophie. "She doesn't want this. She wants the pain to stop. She wants us to..." Sophie choked on her tears. "Let her die."

"We can get her more medicine," said the nurse. "Dr. Wells said there's a chance of…"

"It won't do any good," mumbled Sophie. She dabbed her eyes with her sweatshirt and looked at her mother with all the tubes and drains protruding from her frail body. "She doesn't want to go on like this."

"You may want to talk to Dr. Wells before making that decision," said the nurse.

"He isn't going to change my mind," wept Sophie. "It is what I want…it's what she wants!"

Sophie remained at her mother's side as all life support was removed, and within the hour, Sophie's mother was pronounced dead. While the medical team prepared the body for transport, Sophie stepped into the waiting room and found Dr. Gernsbeck.

"Thank you, doctor," said Sophie with gentle tears still running down her face. "I know now that this was what she wanted, what she needed. Thank you for helping me make the right choice."

"It is patients like your mother who remind me of my oath," said Dr. Gernsbeck. "I solemnly promise that I will serve humanity to the best of my ability – caring for the sick, promoting good health, alleviating pain and suffering. I will assist my patients in making informed decisions that coincide with their own values and beliefs."

Dr. Gernsbeck shook Sophie Verne's hand. "I hope you find peace in the coming days and weeks."

"Because of you and M.E.D.I.U.M., I will," said Sophie and left.

***

Dr. Gernsbeck washed his hands in the doctors' lounge as Dr. Wells approached.

"When will this end, Alphonse," yelled Dr. Wells. "We can barely talk options with the patient's family after you've finished with them."

"My friend, this makes your job easier. You don't have to treat patients who are likely to die soon. No one wants to prolong death," said Dr. Gernsbeck. "Narrowing their options is the simplest solution for today and the future."

Dr. Wells pointed a finger at Dr. Gernsbeck. "But you are lying to the family!"

"I am merely allowing the family to experience their thoughts and emotions projected onto their loved one. They create the images and conversations in the virtual world, not me. The decision to terminate care is always their own. I have not taken that from them but given them the illusion to believe in."

Dr. Wells shook his head. "Such potential, and this is what you choose to use it on."

"It is a small sacrifice today for a bountiful future. For now, I am content with allowing the family to think they see and hear their loved one, even if it is a final farewell."

"It isn't truth. It's objectively a false reality. It's worthless." said Dr. Wells.

"Virtual reality or not, they will see what they want to see. I lead them to believe in a reality where they made the right choice. Surely, that isn't worthless. I take away their fears and grant them peace."

Movie Night

Kerr Pelto

Their Friday dinner and a movie were not to be derailed. It was their special time to unwind and let the week's worth of worries dissipate, that is, if Stella's made-from-scratch pizza suited Frank's finicky palate. She plopped down on the couch facing the blazing fire, threw her cashmere blanket over her legs, and crossed her fingers all would go well.

Frank picked up the remote and chose another disturbing movie, *The Crow*. Stella inhaled a slow, deep breath. Killing sprees did not make for a relaxing evening. Halfway through the movie, Frank paused it to use the bathroom. As time passed, Stella wondered what was taking him so long and was about to check on him when she heard a tapping on the patio door.

"Frank! I heard something. Can you check it out?"

When he didn't answer, Stella got up and opened the sliding glass door. A crow hopped around a lifeless mourning dove on the patio. It flew away as Stella bent down to pick up the beautiful songbird.

Frank crept up behind her. "What do you think you're doing, Stella?"

Startled, Stella almost dropped the tiny creature. "Its body is still warm. Looks like its neck is broken. Poor thing."

"Give it here." Frank took the bird and unceremoniously dumped it in the trash.

"Frank, no! We should bury it in my flower garden."

Frank controlled a sinister smile and retrieved the carcass. "Let's hurry it up. The movie's getting good. Eric's about to kill Tin Tin."

What's getting into him?

Frank rushed the burial and returned to the movie.

The next day, Stella stood at the bay window and watched Frank laugh as he mowed over a baby bird hopping in the grass. Horrified, Stella ran outside and wept over the mangled body.

"Why all the waterworks?"

"Frank, why did you do that?"

"Irritating chirper was already dead." Frank shook his head and continued his chore. He nonchalantly stowed the mower in the garage. Stella stared, dumbfounded. She heaved a silent sigh and wondered if Frank was right. But she could have sworn she saw the chick hopping around.

***

The following Friday, Stella sat at her laptop, chewing her nails, trying to find a recipe for the perfect pizza dough. Frank had remarked her last pizza tasted like cardboard. Once satisfied with her choice, she compiled all the ingredients on the marble countertop. Kneading the dough was therapeutic, and she lost herself in the movements, unaware Frank had slithered up behind her.

His cold hands grabbed her bare shoulders. Caught off guard, she dropped the dough on the floor.

"Frank, don't scare me like that!"

"What are you saying, my little chickadee? Didn't you hear me calling your name?"

Stella shook her head. She must have been too absorbed in the kneading process to hear him.

Frank picked up the dough and set it on the counter. "You seem flighty, Stella. Move over. I'll finish the pizza and get it in the oven." He scooped her up in his arms, carried her to the den, and nestled her gently on the couch cushions. "You're still as light as a feather."

Why is he being so nice?

Just when Stella's nerves had eased, Frank stood in front of her, holding a knife. "Did you cut your finger? There's blood on it."

"I haven't used that knife today."

"Well, you must have." Frank walked back to the sink and threw in the knife. "Next time, wash it."

Stella distinctly recalled not using the knife. Or was that the day before? She agonized over the two days in her mind and felt sure she had never used it.

Frank set the paper plates and slices of pizza on the coffee table, picked up the remote, and clicked on his choice of movie, *Damien: Omen II*. Partway through, he paused the movie to use the bathroom.

What's taking him so long?

Soon, a clicking noise on the sliding glass door unnerved Stella. Standing unsteadily, she approached the door, opened it, and found the crow hopping around a dead mockingbird. Its eyes had been sliced out of their sockets.

Stella's scream froze in her throat; a cold sweat broke out on her brow. Images of Frank holding the bloody knife swirled in a tangled, sickening mess in her head. She swayed and took hold of the door handle.

Frank appeared behind her. "What now?"

In a whisper, she said, "There's another dead bird on the patio."

"I'll bury it." Frank pushed Stella toward the couch. She watched as he walked to the flower garden, pretended to bury it, then flung it over the neighbor's hedge.

Stella met him at the door. "Frank, did you bury it?"

"I said I would, didn't I? Don't be so paranoid. Now, come perch next to me on the sofa."

Frank unpaused the movie and said, "Watch. This is my favorite part. Joan's eyes are about to be pecked out by a raven."

Stella shuddered at the scene and curled up in a ball.

When the night was over, and they were in bed, Frank said, "Time flies when you're having fun, right, babe?" He leaned over and gave Stella a goodnight peck on the cheek.

Stella turned to the wall and wiped the disgusting kiss off her face. Minutes turned to hours until a nightmarish sleep finally crept over her.

***

After Frank left for work the next day, Stella ventured into the neighbor's yard. Not finding the dead bird anywhere, she knelt where he had pretended to bury it in their garden. Noticing a spot with freshly turned-over dirt, she dug her hands in and found it. The hollowed-out eye sockets jolted her. She leaned her head back and wailed, then pummeled the ground with her fists, deflated.

The crow tapped at the sliding glass doors during the days when Stella was home alone. Whenever he showed up, Stella would go outside and talk to him. He became her little feathered friend.

"Hello, Crow. I've made more cookies for you." Stella crumbled the goodies on top of the picnic table. Crow hopped up and down and cawed at her in response. Their time together was Stella's only solace.

"Crow, I have no one else to talk to. I wish you could help me. I'm so confused. I can't sleep at night. I'm wondering if I'm losing my mind. Am I becoming forgetful and seeing things that aren't real? Frank said he buried that bird, and he did. But I could have sworn I saw him throw it into the neighbor's yard."

Crow continued to peck at the crumbs while Stella wept.

***

The following day, Frank drove to work. Stella stood at the window until he was out of sight, then locked the front door. Walking into the master bathroom, she was stunned by her reflection. Her hasty makeup job failed to mask the dark shadows under her eyes. If not for overcaffeinating herself, she'd have no energy at all.

Stella rummaged through Frank's nightstand. Pulling out a dog-eared paperback, she read the title: *Dark Psychology A-Z of Gaslighting*. She ran a nervous hand through her tangled hair and took the book to the patio. As

Frank huffed, "It's that ridiculous bird! I'll take care of him."

Stella jumped off the sofa, ran to the sliding glass door, and opened it. Adrenaline, mixed with fear, propelled her into the torrential rain.

"Go away, Crow! Shoo!"

Crow merely hopped to the edge of the patio.

Without pausing the movie, Frank got up and pushed past Stella onto the patio. "I'm gonna break his scrawny neck with my bare hands!"

Crow cawed. In a cacophonous mass, dozens of crows answered its call and bombarded Frank. He flailed his arms against the assault, lost his balance, and fell backward. The loud cracking of his skull nauseated Stella. Sticky, red blood gushed from a large wound. Frank's dead, hollow eyes stared at Stella. A horrified scream gurgled up from her throat.

The murder of crows aligned themselves on Frank's lifeless body as Crow hopped on his face and hungrily gouged out his eyes.

Wide-eyed, Stella muffled her screams with both hands. As she watched the birds, her worries took flight, and a sense of great calm came over her. From inside the house, Cusack's dying words reverberated in her ears – *May God have mercy on my poor soul.*

A Night Alone

Christopher Bloodworth

"*Shhhhh!* Careful!"

Kayla, whose body was already halfway through a downstairs window of Beau's house, looked up at him in alarm.

"*What?* What do you mean, '*shhhhh?*' You said your parents were gone!"

"They are," he whispered. "But the camera in the foyer sends them alerts when it hears voices. Hence entering through the window instead of the door. Hence *shhhhhh!*"

Kayla rolled her eyes as the slender, sandy-haired boy helped pull her the rest of the way through. Walking backwards, Beau held a quieting finger up to a smile. Pulling her playfully into the kitchen, he opened a high cabinet, and Kayla's mouth fell open at the sea of liquor bottles.

"Holy ... You weren't kidding. They really do have a lot."

"Yeah," whispered Beau, who, having selected and unstoppered a bottle of rum, drank a mouthful of the dark liquid. He screwed up his face and shook his head like a dog shaking off water. "The crazy thing is that they don't even drink anymore. Here."

Kayla grabbed the bottle and took a deep swig, coughed, and imitated Beau's head shake. She'd never had alcohol before but had heard of its supposed ability to calm nerves, and she was certainly nervous about that evening. She swigged again before passing the bottle back.

The teens tiptoed out of the kitchen, up a flight of stairs, and into a room with a king size bed that made Kayla raise her eyebrows.

"Ok, we can talk normally up here," a grinning Beau announced.

Kayla looked around the ornately decorated room.

"Wait, is this your parents' bedroom? Why aren't we in yours?"

"Well, mine's downstairs, but it's by the foyer, so the camera might pick up our voices. You can't hear anything from up here though."

"Oh. Well ... ok." Kayla took another swig from the rum, which was starting to give her an airy kind of feeling. She thought her vision seemed enhanced somehow, as if someone had turned the sharpness slider all the way up. Perhaps it was a placebo, but she was relieved to find that the rum seemed to be helping her nerves. Kayla glanced around and picked up an expensive-looking painted glass vase from atop a dresser.

"Wooow, your parents' stuff is *so* nice!"

"Haha yeah ... That's kind of one of my dad's favorite pieces though, so maybe just put that back."

"Oh. Oops." She pronounced the "oops" with extra o's as she replaced the vase haphazardly.

Kayla was basking in the silliness quickly taking the place of her nerves, and she felt little restraint as she began opening drawers, pulling out undergarments with a giggle. Beau looked bemused but didn't stop her.

"Uh, whatcha doing? You know I have to clean all that up before my parents get back in town, right?"

"*Shhhhh.* I'm snooping."

"Riiight." Beau put the cap back on the rum. "So I think we're all done with the rum. There's a delay from when you drink it and when it gets in your bloodstream, so the sensation's only gonna keep building."

"Aww. But I like the sensation. But ok, I'll trust you," she said before brightening. "Come on, help me out. I'm looking for your parents' sex things."

"Ew, gross. I don't want to find that."

"Whoa, look at this!"

Kayla delicately held up a shiny black pistol she'd pulled from the bedside table.

"Whoa! Kayla?" Beau used a balanced tone you might adopt to coax a toddler into handing over scissors. "Any chance you want to put that back? Maybe? Please?"

"Sorry," she apologized, showing more presence of mind as she returned the gun to the drawer. "Why the eff do your parents have this here anyway?"

Beau shrugged, "It's my mom's. It's for break-ins, and I'm definitely *not* allowed to touch it."

"Riiight." Kayla rolled her eyes, but quickly regretted it—Beau was now looking decidedly uncomfortable on the other side of the bed. "Well ... anyway, forget it. I shouldn't have snooped." He didn't respond other than to shrug. Wanting very much to shift the mood, Kayla tried to adopt a fiery look and bit her bottom lip. "So ... should we do this?"

Beau looked up, a little surprised, but he couldn't suppress a smile.

"What, just like that?"

Kayla kicked off her shoes suggestively. Crawling towards him on all fours across the bed, she leaned over and whispered, "Just ... like ... that," and lightly nibbled the edge of his ear.

Beau closed his eyes in anticipation and melted beneath her. Not bothering to remove clothes, the two wrapped themselves in each other's limbs. They kissed passionately, and it wasn't long before their hands were exploring, searching out those coveted prizes—holy grails of hormonal youths.

As Beau slipped a hand down past her belly button and under the elastic of Kayla's shorts, she reached out of habit to pull his hand away—a much-practiced tradition of their physical relationship. Typically, there was seemingly no end to the number of such attempts Beau was willing to make, but as she pulled his hand back this time, she felt his body tense a little, and she realized that he was no longer kissing her back.

"What's wrong?"

Beau lifted himself into a seated position and shrugged.

"Is it because I stopped you? That was just out of habit." She grabbed his hand and put it over her shorts. "It's ok—you can touch me there."

Beau pulled his hand from hers. Kayla looked like she'd been slapped. His eyes moved to her, around the room, and then back down.

"Maybe now's not the right time," he shrugged again.

Kayla scoffed.

"For real? This whole thing was your idea."

"I don't know ... maybe it was the gun; maybe it's the alcohol ..." he glanced over at a family portrait. "Maybe it's being in my parents' bedroom? I'm just in a weird headspace."

"Fine." Kayla stood up and grabbed her shoes. "Whatever."

Beau looked at her in surprise.

"Look," she said irritably, "I'm gonna walk home, and you can just sit up here and mope or whatever you'd rather be doing without me."

"*What?* I didn't say—Kayla, wait."

But, despite an intoxicated unsteadiness, Kayla was already halfway down the stairs. Beau jumped out of the bed, hoarsely whispering her name as he bounded down the staircase after her.

"*Kayla!* Wait, please!"

She'd reached the kitchen before turning around, allowing him to catch up and grab her hands. He sighed deeply before continuing in a quiet whisper.

"Look, I'm sorry," he said, relieved to see her hard look soften a little. "I just got in my own—"

CRASH!

The teens looked around in alarm at the sound of broken glass, instinctively moving closer together.

"Beau? What was that?"

"It ... it sounded like someone broke a window."

"Oh my God." Kayla covered a gasp with her hands, her eyes already glistening as she sank to the floor. Her heart was beating so loud that she could hardly hear. Why had she drunk all that rum? "Beau, call 911."

"Hold on." Though whispering, Beau tried to sound firm and in control, "We don't know anything yet. We can't call 911 just because we heard a scary noise."

"Beau, someone is literally *breaking into* this house!"

"Let's just—everything's gonna be fine. Here's what we're gonna do. We're gonna go to the bedroom—my mom's gun's in there. We'll be safe. Everything's ... everything is going to be fine."

"Like *hell* am I going upstairs. The sound *came* from there!"

Beau shook his head, pointing out of a doorway in the kitchen "It sounded like it came from my dad's office. We'll be safe upstairs."

Kayla shook her head resolutely. Beau looked back and forth between Kayla and the bedroom before making up his mind.

"Ok, I'm going for the gun. Stay here, and don't make a sound."

"Beau, no!"

"I'll be right back. Just stay low and wait here."

With that, Beau disappeared, leaving Kayla utterly alone.

Tears fell unbidden from her eyes as Kayla looked around the kitchen. She felt that everything before her was humming with a vibrant intensity. It was as though the world were vibrating at such a frequency as to create the illusion of stillness. How long had she stood there? She tried listening for the sound of Beau on the stairs or of creaking floorboards, but it was no use. All she could hear was the overwhelming thud of her own heartbeat. Beau should be back by now. Or had he just left? As long as she stood still, the flow of time seemed unmeasurable to Kayla, and she determined that only by moving could she take her fate into her own hands.

Kayla's stomach turned as she crawled on all fours, inching around the kitchen island until she could reach the knife block. She grabbed a carving knife and sat against the cabinets, clutching the knife to her chest with both hands as she heaved. She wanted to throw up. Where was Beau? Should she call out for him? No. *He's ok*, she thought. But was he? She had been sure the glass breaking had come from the direction of the stairs. Could he have been ambushed? *Everything's gonna be fine*, she repeated Beau's words to herself. Maybe he had to load the gun? Did that take a long time? Kayla didn't know.

All she knew was that illusion of stillness was breaking down, the room spinning around her as she tumbled helplessly like sheets in a dryer. The kitchen was too big. She needed somewhere confined to stop the spinning—a bathroom, a closet ... *a pantry*! On the other side of the kitchen, she could see her haven. She just had to move. She just had to—

Bang!

Bang!

Kayla screamed. The gunshots had frozen time. Two shots. Beau was dead. He'd shot first, then been shot. And she would be next. Would it be long? She needed to hide. She needed to call 911.

Kayla did her best to crawl to the pantry. At the sound of gunshots, the room had stopped spinning around her, but she now seemed to be tumbling through it of her own accord. Holding the knife in one hand, she reached with her other to pull out her phone. It fell to the floor, and she couldn't seem to pick it up. Why wouldn't her hands work? She pushed it along in front of her for an interminable amount of time before reaching the pantry, closing the door behind her. The killer would find her soon. How much time did she have?

Kayla didn't bother fumbling to pick her phone up. It seemed to be all she could do just to punch 911 and press her ear to the phone on the floor.

"911, what is the nature of your emergency?"

Shit! Why hadn't she realized she would have to speak?

"Hello? There's an intruder in my boyfriend's house. He's been shot. I'm—"

"Ma'am, can you give me the address? Ma'am?"

But Kayla wasn't listening. With her face to the ground, she felt it—the footsteps that stopped on the other side of the door. She was about to die, but she would die resisting. It took everything she had to fight the inebriation, but she pulled herself to her feet, still clutching the carving knife. The handle turned. Kayla screamed, instinctively closing her eyes as the door opened.

"Kayla? It's ... *wait—*"

Beau stepped back, a shocked look on his face as his hand fumbled for the carving knife in his side. Slowly, he dropped to the floor, Kayla screaming again—this time in horror over her mistake.

Kayla was in no condition to make her way upstairs, but if she had, she might have found the source of the confusion—the broken glass vase on the floor, which had fallen after a time, as things do, after she'd set it down precariously on the edge of the dresser. Beau, in a dark twist of fate, hadn't noticed the shattered glass on his father's side of the bedroom. Instead, he'd retrieved his mother's loaded gun and, inexperienced with firearms, discharged it twice in his search for the safety.

Downstairs, Kayla sank beside Beau, placing her hands uselessly against his side as the operator repeated her questions, "Ma'am? Ma'am, are you still there?"

The Path of Totality

Bryn Eliesse

Crickets chirped as the little boy climbed. Umbar's pudgy hands fiddled with the edge of his shirt, running a finger over the dinosaur ducky on the silicon surface. The stone stairs ended, and his dark-suited guard, who had been leading the stumbling boy up the stairs, pushed open a door to an office. Umbar squinted up at the sign on the door.

Dr. Emil Qumarim, MD, WzD, PhD

Tired of the child's dawdling, the guard simply decided to shove the small boy into the room—

Umbar let out a squeak as his red sneakers caught the edge of a rug. Just before he hit the floor, a wrinkled hand wrapped around his upper arm with a strong grip, righting him on his feet. Giddy with the rush of adrenaline, Umbar smiled up into his savior's cold face, his smile bright despite the ice in the psychiatrist's purple irises. Instead of fussing, the child patted the psychiatrist's surprisingly warm hand and looked around the room to find his seat.

Two dinky chairs sat across from a big important-looking one. And smack in the middle was a tiny chair just for him! Toddling across the room, he plopped in the seat and began to play with his shirt again, half listening to the adults. Only when the guard yelled did Umbar turn to listen.

"But sir! You don't mean for me to leave him here, do you?"

Umbar tilted his head in fascination, pausing his legs mid-swing. The psychiatrist's trim-cut hair and beard fluffed like Umbar's favorite cat until it settled into a tidy style again. With a growly, grumpy sort of voice, his new silvery friend, Em, replied, "Of course I do. I may be old, but I have been in practice since you were in diapers. I have no need for your services."

Umbar bit his lip, trying to stop the giggle bubbling out of him. Finally, he had to cover his mouth with his hands to keep from laughing when the guard's face turned red. Umbar knew no laughing was allowed; the fancy men in dark suits always got mad when he laughed.

"You can't mean–"

Em's face was hard as he drawled, "I will call for you when we are finished." A strong gale had Umbar bouncing in his seat with glee as the wind promptly pushed his guard out the door without another word and slammed it behind him. "Well then." Em straightened the feather quill in his breast pocket and turned to the boy.

Both hands over his mouth did nothing to hide the pure joy shining from Umbar's dark eyes. With a put-upon sigh, the psychiatrist said, "Go ahead."

Thus, Umbar burst into a high-pitched bout of raving while Em picked up a kettle from the dragon-leg table beside the leatherback chair. Umbar babbled, recounting the events with glee, "And then whoosh! Suit man was gone! I have never–"

With a careful eye, Dr. Emil Qumarim, or for all of Umbar's purposes—Em, fiddled around his office making tea while observing the child. With both front teeth missing, each of the boy's words was enunciated with a clearly defined lisp. Tiny hands twisted and caressed his t-shirt unconsciously as he spoke, his red shoes kicking back and forth beneath him.

The boy's demeanor did not surprise the man. After a century or two in practice, very few things surprised Dr. Emil Qumarim—that is to say, it is not every day that a demi-astral stumbled into his office, much less one as lethal as Emil was forewarned this bubbly child had been.

As the warm scent of bergamot wafted into the air, Emil settled into his chair with a quiet sigh. The psychiatrist cleared his throat before taking a long sip. Umbar fell silent, staring up at Em with a wide, curious gaze.

"Do you know why you're here today?"

"Yup," Umbar replied, popping the 'p'. The sounds of crickets grew louder. "Talk about my feelings, right?"

"That would be correct. Particularly about your parents." The same parents who had passed a year prior. Dr. Emil watched with bated breath for the darkness to stir in the boy's eyes.

Umbar grew deathly still. A small pout formed with puckered lips on his soft face. The tinkling birdsong coming through the open window faded to silence. "No, thank you."

"And why is that?" Emil pursued in a mild voice.

Umbar looked out the window and shook his head, so the man repeated the question in the same careful tone. Tears sparkled on the Umbar's dark lashes, "Because I don't wanna."

Emil sipped his tea before taking a shallow breath. "Why?"

A single shrug.

"Would they not want you to?"

Something moved behind Umbar's dark eyes. "How would I know? They're gone. So nothing I say is gonna help them anyways."

"Then what would you like to talk about?"

Umbar perked up in his seat as if no one had asked him this question before. Silent for a few seconds, he scanned the room before pointing to the bookshelf, "What's that for?"

"My late mentor's cauldron. What once was used for magnificent spells has now been shrunken down for tea, I am afraid. Nothing too interesting."

The psychiatrist relented for the next hour or so, which dissolved into explanations of his items and riveting discussions of the merits of Umbar's favorite toys. The wizened man watched the boy with some wariness, but the enthusiasm of the boy was infectious. Emil decided the deeper questions could wait for their next session.

Umbar watched with some satisfaction as Emil let him talk about what *he* wanted to talk about. In these places, everyone always yelled at him until he made them go away. He didn't want to do that to this man. Em was nice, even if he didn't look it. *Even his face which had been so cold was much warmer now, as he explained another one of his shelf thingies!* Umbar thought, as Em explained another of his shelf thingies. The coldness started to come back as Em shifted in his seat; Em's purple gaze fell upon the yellow flower on his table that was curling in sleep. *The flowers always go to sleep though,* Umbar puzzled.

The flower was the key for the psychiatrist. Emil didn't know what had woken the boy's sacred spirit, only that he had just under three minutes. The darkness was motionless, but the flower alerted the wizened man to his immediate peril. Three minutes, yet he could not tear his eyes away from the boy, even as his flesh prickled and broke out in bumps.

Confusion muddled the child's expression, with his plump lips pursed in a pout. And the two stared. Stared at each other until the man could see the thing of darkness swimming behind the child's eyes. Emil's mouth went dry. Umbar swung his feet again, gazing intently into the psychiatrist's gaze, unblinking, like it was a game. Every few seconds, when the old man blinked, Umbar gleefully called out that he had won, and the game started again.

Umbar grew more and more still, swinging shoes coming to a halt. His giggles faded into a terse silence leaving only the crickets' piercing song beyond the window and the crackling crunch of the wilting flower, now brown and crumbling to dust. The shadows of the shelves grew long, reaching for the silent child. The sun's light obscured; the room dimmed. All the while, Umbar only stared with a lingering smile on his lips.

In the child's dark gaze, a form began to take shape—the gaping maw of a creature with a lolling tongue dripping in a thick dark stream. What surprised Emil was not the creature, but the childlike glee shining in its wide gaze. It struck the aged man then—he was just a game, its new playmate, on the Path of Totality.

The screaming of the crickets faded into a final silence. As the light faded from the silvery man, the psychiatrist remembered the whispered words of his mentor from oh so long ago. *Remember—you mustn't look, for even a second, into an astral abyss.*

Logs

Séimí Mac Aindreasa

Frayed scarlet ribbons of skin peeled away as, yet again, his family came to visit the log cabin. His bulging stomach split open, revealing moss-glistening bowel, gorged with crawling maggots and reeking of decay and preservative. As wraithlike forms screamed in silence around the edges of his snowy bed, small, white hands pushed through the chaos of organs, clawing their way out through his abdomen.

He knew he should feel pain, yet as the tiny, porcelain fingers tore skin and cracked bone in their efforts to escape, he felt a comforting warmth at the mutilation. This was only the beginning; the rest would be here soon.

"...Isamu..."

His name, whispered on a non-existent breeze in a familiar voice etched with pain and sorrow.

"Isamu...Where are you?"

Isamu clutched the bedclothes tightly as the first tendrils of fear crawled, insect-like, from the charred log walls, dropping to the floor with wet, heavy plops. The floor, already slick with dark, viscous matter, rippled slowly, as if disturbed by forms moving beneath, leaving oily wavelets in their wake.

Beads of stinging sweat formed on his clammy forehead and trickled down his face. Despite the growing heat, his feet felt intensely cold. Glancing down fearfully, he saw the nails, stark bright against the festering, blue-black ruin of his toes.

"...Isamu – where are you? Why aren't you here?"

"I...I am here! I'm right here!"

His voice sounded weak, unsure. The sweat began to burn, blistering the delicate skin below his eyes. He tried to blink, yet his eyelids would not close. They could not waste a second of this precious time.

"Oto-san? Father?"

Isamu watched as a cracked, blackened hand and arm snaked from beneath his bed. Angry red scars split and opened as the small, charred fingers groped across the crisp, white sheets, dribbling greyish-yellow fluid across the clean linen. The surrounding wraiths churned in silent anguish as the burned digits scratched onwards. A blotched and scabrous head began to rise, and Isamu felt tears of fear, joy and fathomless sadness well-up in his burning eyes. The small hands in his belly clenched and grasped in excitement, breaking ribs in their eagerness. Still, he felt no pain. Only warmth and love.

Scorched black holes fixed him in their unseeing gaze atop a misshapen nose, wrinkled and sagging in a face which seemed to have melted into the scrawny neck below.

"Ichika," Isamu laughed. "Beautiful Ichika, more lovely than ten thousand flowers!"

As Isamu reached out to the seared form climbing onto the bed, his hand brushed against something cold and hard at his side. His heart quickened as his eyes tracked to the doll which lay there, its painted face a mosaic of fractured porcelain; blank eyes staring accusingly.

"Wánjù wáwá. Chǐrǔ." *Doll. Shame.* The words were stilted and coarse in his own language. He made to lift the doll, to cast it from him and smash it against the – the logs. But the logs stared at him accusingly. He could almost hear their questions: Would you do this? Would you go this far? Would you take this final step, beyond any last hope of peace and redemption?

His hand stayed, as always. This was his punishment. The burden he must carry with him in exchange for the brief respite given him by the visitations.

The hand, lifted to throw, lowered to softly caress the doll. As it did so, the logs settled, the ghostly shapes retreating into their soundless agony. Looking down, he saw the form in his gut and the blackened thing sitting at the foot of the bed, watching him in silence. His face softened, and he asked in mock reproval, "Where is your brother?"

Even as he spoke, a shadow moved on the wall. Darkness shifted, detached. A black, shifting form, in the shape of a tall boy, peeled itself from the inky background and silently approached the bed. On the wall, the hole left in its absence filled with the swirling mass of inconsequential shapes.

Asahi. Sunlight. Yet a light, brighter than the sun, had transformed him, raised him to another plane. Asahi, who had once held Isamu's future in his heart and in his strong hands. Now, he was as much a prisoner here as Isamu; in this prison of logs, each one cut by Isamu's own callousness.

Isamu cradled the gaping tear in his midriff and looked at each visitor in turn, a warm smile on his face.

"Someone is missing. Where is she?"

As he spoke, a soft, crackling sound came from one dark corner. Smiling ruefully, Isamu leaned forward as slowly, a shape began to emerge from the smoky gloom. Wraiths swirled around it, attempting to hold it back.

"No!" Isamu shouted. "You must let her through! That is the agreement!"

The shapes twisted and curled angrily around the new creature before withdrawing, allowing her to come into view.

Sepia-tinted, cracked and creased as if folded and unfolded time and again, she approached the bed. The true rising sun in Isamu's blighted existence. Kazuko. As beautiful as the day he had taken her photograph.

"Husband? Where are you? Isamu?"

"I am here, my wife. We are all here." Isamu smiled as his family gathered around the bed.

"We should give her a name," Isamu whispered, indicating the small shape nestling in the open wound in his festering intestines.

"No! No name! Too soon!"

Kazuko's voice seemed to drift through the air as if from a long way off, buffeted by winds. Isamu nodded. Always the same suggestion. Always the same reply.

"Very well, my dear. In time, in time. Come, my family. Come closer."

Isamu sat up in bed and spoke quietly.

"I promise you: soon I will be free of this log prison, and I will be with you all again, for*ever*."

"When?" Kazuko wailed, causing the spirit forms to ripple and twist agitatedly. "When? So cold! So frightened! So lonely!"

The same pleas and questions. The same responses. His hand subconsciously closed around the doll beside him.

"When they decide I have paid my penance and have earned peace, my loves. Only then will I be able to leave this place. Only then will we be reunited."

The hand caressed the cold ceramic face of the doll, his thumb feeling the smooth round contours. Ashamed, he released the toy and pushed it away, but not too far away.

As if in response, the haze around the bed thickened to a dark smog. The slick floor began to undulate, fat bubbles churning on its greasy surface.

Misty tendrils wrapped themselves around Ichika, Asahi and Kazuko, dragging them away from the bed. The forever-unnamed baby was enveloped in mist, Isamu's belly already beginning to close over.

"No! It's too soon! Please!" Isamu knew it was pointless. Tearfully, he watched his family be pulled away into the smoky ether, smothered by the unforgiving entities. Isamu sobbed as the shapeless sentinels of his log prison slowly and silently withdrew into their wooden walls. Dripping walls and glutinous floor gradually solidified.

"Tomorrow. They will return tomorrow," he whimpered to himself through laboured breath.

As they finally closed in sleep, Isamu's eyes glimpsed a sterile, white room, harshly lit by fluorescent lighting. Machines beeped and purred, and two faces stared at him through a window in the door.

Tomorrow night.

"What's wrong with him? Who is he?"

"Don't you know? That's Isamu Ishikawa! The Manshu Monster? Ishii's Executioner? He was a guard at Unit 731 in Manchuria during the war. I read somewhere that he killed hundreds of Chinese, mainly women and children!"

"The war? He must be a hundred!"

"Ninety-six, actually. He's been here for almost thirty years. He was transferred from Fuchū Prison in 1975 when he started displaying – unusual behaviour."

"The crying and pleading?"

"There's a bit more to it than that. Unit 731 was disbanded as the war ended. Most were captured and tried, with many executions. Ishikawa escaped and made his way home – to Hiroshima. There, he found that his family: son, daughter and pregnant wife, had been killed in the blast. He was captured when he was approached by occupation forces and asked for identification. He immediately told them everything about himself. His trial was a formality. He admitted to every charge and was imprisoned for life."

"What a monster! Why is he allowed to live?"

"It's that respect for the elders thing, isn't it? It doesn't matter that he murdered people: he's Rōjin, so must be respected. It's weird though. When he was captured, he was carrying a photograph of his wife and a Chinese doll, a Wánjù wáwá – pardon the pronunciation. Nothing would make him give it up. He broke a guard's arm, when they tried to remove it. That's the doll on the bed, beside him. They think it came from the camp; possibly from one of the inmates."

"It must have been an awful shock, though, to find your entire family was dead."

"I suppose so. It's probably for the best that he believed they were dead, in the long run."

"What do you mean? They all died. You said so yourself."

"Ah, that's what they thought at the time. But the daughter survived. She was blinded – her eyes were destroyed by the blast – and she was badly burned, but she lived."

"Did he know that?"

"No. It was decided not to tell him. No point in making things worse. He'd probably try to escape, and he's not fit enough for that."

"Yeah, you're right. He's better off in his safe place, his – what did he call it? His log cabin."

"Yes – his 'log cabin'. All those prisoners they tortured, raped, mutilated, vivisected, burned, froze and tore apart? Do you know what they called them?

They called them 'Logs'."

Mercy and Death

Jonathan Braunstein

Nothing ever happened in Eastmeadow, a sleepy little town in the Midwest, until the unexplained murders began.

Frank Parsons, the school's janitor and sole eyewitness, went about his daily cleaning routine. As he filled the bucket to mop the floors, Frank fumbled for the thing ringing in his pocket. The smartphone always felt too large for his hands. He held it up at arm's length, and after three attempts managed to swipe right to answer the unknown caller. "Hello? Hello, I'm sorry. I can't hear you! Hello?"

As he struggled with his phone, a puddle quickly grew at his feet. "Gosh dang it, the water!" Frank turned the faucet off before the spill got worse, and as he dry-mopped the floor, he suddenly remembered the call and raised the phone to his ear. "Hello there! Hello?" There was no reply.

The final bell chimed and students began crowding the hallways.

Frank instinctively closed the janitor's closet to allow for the main hallway traffic. The students were the reason he loved his job of fifty years; as they walked by, he smiled and waved, but no one took notice... except Chloe.

"Good afternoon, Chloe. How is seventh grade treating you?"

"Hey, Gramps! Your light is on."

He turned the light toward his face to look and squinted in the brightness. "Oh, this darned thing. How do I turn it off?"

"You see that circle in the corner? If you press it, it works the flashlight when your phone is locked." She pressed the icon, and the light went out.

"I'm not sure I understand what any of that means, but once again, you're my savior, young lady. Send my regards to Charlene."

"Yep! I'll say hi to Grandma for you." She started to walk away but then swung around, pointing at Frank. "You like my grandma, don't you?"

Leaning on his mop handle and trying to look suave, Frank said, "You think I still got a chance with the ladies?" He rubbed his scruffy chin.

"You bet you do!"

Frank watched as she skipped down the hallway and joined her friends on their way out. He didn't have the heart to tell Chloe he would never get over his Vivian. She was the love of his life. If he had only let her know more often during the fifty years they were together before her passing.

Down the hallway, Frank noticed a bald man wearing a black gym suit with a misguided high school boy named Dylan. The man placed his lanky fingers on the boy's shoulder. Dylan stepped back, swatted the man's hand away, and scoffed at him.

Who's that man? Frank stepped forward to talk with the stranger, but he darted around the corner. By the time

Frank got there, the man was gone.

Frank asked, "Dylan, who was that man?"

"Some creeper or something. He, like, whispered something in my ear."

Alarmed even more by this stranger, Frank went to the teachers, but none seemed concerned. He decided to dismiss it.

Soon after the hallways were empty, peace once again settled in the building without a living soul to be found. Frank straightened each classroom accordingly, checking off each task from his list, and made sure they were ready for the next day.

***

Early the next morning, Frank was rudely awakened by someone banging on the front door. His bones creaked as he got out of bed. The banging continued. Frank hollered, "All right, all right, I'm coming!"

A policeman shifted his feet awkwardly. "Sir, I'm sorry to bother you. We, uh, tried calling. We have some questions."

"Questions? About what? And don't call me *sir*. I've known you your whole life, Steven Metcalf."

"Okay, Frank. I'll shoot straight with you. A young man was found dead behind the school yesterday evening. According to the time log and surveillance cameras, you and the boy were the only ones on the school grounds at the time of his death."

Frank held his hand to his mouth and shuddered. "This... this is horrible. Please come in." He showed him to the living room.

Steven looked around the room. Although it was neat, an inch of dust covered everything. "You clean the school every day. What about your home?"

"I know. I know. Vivian would be ashamed. I just don't have the heart to move anything since... since I lost her."

"It's been what? A year now?"

Frank teared up. "Yes."

"I'm sorry for your loss. Frank, they want me to take you in for questioning. The boy's death is eerily similar to your wife's and on exactly the same day one year later."

Frank might have been slow with technology, but he was still sharp concerning people. "I've got nothing to hide. Ask anything you want, young man, right here and now."

The officer took out a notepad. "The boy in question is Dylan Harris. Did you see anything suspicious or out of the ordinary at the school last night?"

"I did see something, but not last night. An older gentleman, wearing black. I didn't recognize him."

"What did you see?"

"He was talking with Dylan after school in the hallway. I thought maybe it was a relative from out of town or something. Anyway, Dylan kinda shrugged the guy off and the man ran away."

"Can you describe this man?"

"Yeah... He's of slight build and, uhh, he's not much taller than I am. Definitely bald, but I wasn't very close, so I can't tell you his eye color or nothing."

Steven scribbled down the description. "Was there anyone else who might have seen him to corroborate your story?"

"One of the teachers or students surely must have."

"I'll check the surveillance cameras. What else can you offer me? Know any details about a struggle they had outside? Maybe you heard something from inside when you were working? Did you hear a scream?"

"I told you. I don't know anything about what happened to the boy. Not sure if this matters, and I know it's only a rumor, but I heard that Dylan might have fallen in with the wrong crowd, if you know what I mean. With them drugs and stuff."

"Thank you, Frank. You've been very helpful. I'll call you if I need anything further."

***

School was canceled due to Dylan's death, so Frank took the opportunity to visit Vivian's grave. He thought about the stranger wearing black and who he was the entire way. He knelt by Vivian's grave, gently removed the carnations he left the week before, and placed fresh chrysanthemums in their stead.

"Viv, I don't know if you can hear me, but I miss you. I love you. I can't believe you've been gone for a year." He wiped tears from his eyes, and his voice quivered as he spoke, "A boy died last night, and I feel like I shoulda done something. I don't know if I did right. If you were here, you'd have the right words to make me feel better."

A raspy voice from behind commented, "It's the anniversary of her death, isn't it, Frank?" Despite the hiss, there was something comforting behind the words.

Frank responded, almost to himself without thinking, while he stared blankly at her headstone, "She just stopped breathing. She wasn't even sick. No one saw it coming. I felt like I must have missed something somehow."

A shadow loomed over him. "I have something to tell you."

Frank looked over his shoulder and saw the man he had seen in the hallway. His unexplained calm became unease. "Oh, it's you. I saw you talking with Dylan. Who are you?"

"You can tell them Dylan struggled when the life was choked out of him. Many don't fight as hard as he did. Vivian didn't."

Frank's breath became shallow with frozen fright, temples pulsed with boiling anger. Regaining his composure, he subtly patted his pockets to find his smartphone.

"What do you intend to do, Frank? Call the police?"

Frank turned around. "They're looking for you. I told them about you!"

The man didn't react. "There's no evidence I was there. That's how it works. And if you're wondering... your precious Viv only whimpered at the end. She begged for it to end."

"What is this? Are you just here to torture me? Some cruel game?"

"You want to know my game? Very well. Meet me tonight at the bingo hall."

Frank's cell phone rang and buzzed. This time he swiped correctly and put the phone to his ear. "Hello?"

"Frank, this is Steven. No one saw a man in black at the school, and there's nothing on the cameras. I've redirected my attention to Dylan's friends, but it's not looking good. Please consider coming to the station. We'll take some DNA and clear this whole thing up and get you off the radar, so to speak. The sergeant is really pressuring me."

"You tell your damned sergeant, Charlie Patterson, that I'm not a suspect. I know where the man is. He's right here."

"Right where, Frank?"

"Right here at the cemetery!" Frank looked up, but all he saw were old forgotten headstones and one freshly dug grave. "I'm telling you. He was right here. I can't believe it. After confessing to killing Dylan and Vivian..." He murmured incoherently as he frantically looked around him.

"Frank? Frank? What are you saying? Are you okay? Did the man hurt you?"

Frank sighed and rubbed his eyes, momentarily unsure of his own sanity.

"Dispatch, send an officer to the cemetery now."

"No, no, Steven. Everything is okay. I'm okay. The man must have left when I answered the phone and... anyway, he said he'll meet me at the bingo game tonight."

"Bingo? Okay, Frank, I'm giving you some latitude here because I know you and you've been through a lot. I'll be there at the game tonight before it starts. I'll grab what officers I can, and we'll be watching for any strangers and unusual activity. I want you to go tonight like he said, but don't talk with me or anyone. Subtly signal me when you get there and again when you see him. You're the only witness to this potential suspect. Do you understand what I am saying, and do you have any questions?"

"What if he tries something? What should I do?"

"Don't do anything. Leave that to me."

"I understand, Steven. Thank you." Frank knew this whole thing sounded crazy, but figured a police presence tonight was a good thing.

***

Frank sat in the middle of the room across from Charlene, Chloe's grandma, in the Bingo Hall. He arranged his bingo cards in a row to appear like he was playing and waited. He gave a small nod at Steven, who was standing by the main entrance. A young cadet was casually leaning against the wall, flirting with the girl behind the concessions stand next to him.

Stale smoke hung in the air, and a low murmur came forth from the crowd. The balls spun in the machine with a whir, and soft bounces reverberated through the hall. The monotone voice of the caller droned out "B-12."

Frank was entranced by the dance of the bingo balls. He imagined each one being unaware of its turn until it hit the pneumatic tube.

"N-32."

Frank didn't notice the bald man until he was already seated across from him.

This time, the man was wearing a black pin-striped suit. "I love games of chance! Don't you, Frank?"

Frank abruptly stood up, accidentally knocking his metal seat over. It clapped and clanged as it hit the floor.

The room fell silent, minus the bingo balls ricocheting off the plexiglass and each other. All eyes stared at Frank.

"Now now, Frank. Before you say or do anything you'll regret, sit. You're the only one who can see or hear me."

Frank picked up his chair and sat. "Sorry, everyone..." He furrowed his brow and narrowed his eyes at the man in disbelief.

The man stood on the top of the table and screamed at the top of his lungs, "Can you see me, folks? Whoo! Someone is dying tonight!" He kept his arms outstretched as he stepped down.

No one responded. The room reconvened its low chatter as the Bingo game continued.

"O-73."

"See? Nobody knows I'm here... except you, Frank."

Frank slumped back. "No, this can't be right."

Charlene leaned over. She whispered, "It's okay. There will be more games after this one. You can only win once, anyway. Makes it more exciting, don't you think? One chance is all you ever get."

"Here's *my game,* Frank. I'm a harbinger. I appear to announce one's imminent death. Yesterday, I merely told Dylan he was going to die, and he did. Isn't it mercy to let someone know they have little time left?"

"I-29."

"You still don't believe me? I'll demonstrate. Excuse me, Charlene?" He playfully tapped her on the hand. "I have good news for you! You're about to win seventy-five dollars, and soon after, you will die a painful death."

"G-60."

She looked up. "Oh, you shocked me. Didn't see you there. I'm sorry, son, I'm hard of hearing. Did you say I'm going to win?"

"I certainly did, Charlene. Tonight, you've been chosen."

She looked down. "I have Bingo? Bingo!" She squeezed the man's hand. "You must be my lucky charm. I've played for years, and I've never won!"

The Harbinger winked and cracked a sharp-toothed grin. "Tonight's your lucky night."

Frank watched as Charlene shuffled to the caller to confirm her winning numbers. "I *will* stop you."

"No, you can't. Once someone's number is called, once they've been told, it's too late."

Frank looked him square in the eye. "She couldn't hear you. So, was she actually told?"

The Harbinger chuckled. "Getting philosophical now, Frank? Enjoy the rest of your game."

Charlene came bounding back and grabbed Frank's arm. "I can't believe I won seventy-five dollars!"

Frank looked, but the Harbinger was once again gone.

"Where'd that sweet man go?"

"I don't know, Charlene. And he's not so sweet."

***

When the last Bingo game was called, the hall began to empty. The cadet left his post by the concessions, and Frank noticed Steven was making his way through the octogenarian crowd. He suspected he might be arrested, but he didn't care. After offering to walk her home, Frank stuck close to her side. He would not let Charlene die.

As they walked through the crowd, Frank looked around for any sign of the Harbinger. When he glanced to the left, someone bumped Charlene from the right and she dropped her prize. It fell right into Frank's hands.

She snatched the money from his grasp. "Frank, did you try to steal my money?"

"No, Charlene. I would never."

"Chloe said you were nice, but now... I'm not so sure. I'll walk myself home, thank you." She scurried away through the back entrance.

Frank pursued after her, crashing through the heavy door and into the darkness of the night.

"Get away from me!" Charlene screamed.

"I didn't try to take your money. I'm just trying to protect you."

"No! Frank? Help m—" Charlene's voice faltered as she gasped for air.

Frank held his phone up.

How do I turn this blasted thing on? He tapped the flashlight icon, but nothing happened.

"...nooooo," she wheezed.

He pressed on the symbol, and the flashlight lit.

Charlene was suspended four feet high against the building's brick wall, her arms and legs splayed. She gasped for air, each breath shorter than the last.

Frank nearly fainted as she struggled, and he breathed in deep, as if it would help. Despite his fear, he dared not look away and moved closer.

Charlene lifted her head up as she battled for breath. When she could fight no longer, she fell from the wall and crashed to the ground.

Frank quickly came to her side and listened to see if she was breathing.

Steven came running and saw Charlene on the ground with Frank over her.

***

Frank didn't sleep. He sat up all night, shoulders slumped, his mind running through scenarios of what he could have done differently.

When the light of sunrise peeked through the cell window, a visitor appeared, wearing black priestly garb. He sat down next to Frank.

Frank didn't lift his head. "I figured you'd come."

"You'll be here a very long time, Frank. Being accused of three deaths, all by choking? I can help... if you'd like. Would you like me to?"

"Are you saying that you'll confess?"

The Harbinger lifted Frank's chin and forced him to look into his dark eyes. "Would you like me to tell you that you're gonna die today, Frank? Be with your precious Vivian? Or you and I can continue this game. I'll follow you, telling others they're going to die. You'll try to stop me, knowing you can't win? The choice is yours."

Frank thought long and hard about it before sighing and whispering his reply.

The Harbinger grinned.

Nobody Talks to the Grimm Reaper

Mikayla Hill

Grimm feigned patience as he waited for the morning's meeting to be over. The clacking of his fingers, as they drummed against the table, provided a rhythmic backdrop to the supervisor's droning announcements.

"Now remember: we trust you, as reapers, to make informed decisions when there is a life-or-death choice. You need to ascertain your target has died *before* you remove their soul. I'm looking at you, Todd. Dismissed."

The assembled reapers dispersed, heading out for their respective collections. Grimm stood as he picked up his sheet and, strolling toward the door, looked through the list of names; only five today. Before he could leave, his supervisor pulled him aside.

"You're the best in my team, Grimm. You have made no mistakes, collected all the souls we have asked of you, and made good judgements in those occasional life-or-death calls. Keep it up and you'll have my job in no time."

That was the last thing he wanted, and he couldn't help but grimace; however, without flesh, it was easily mistaken for a grin.

His supervisor smiled, clapping him on the back. "That's the spirit!"

Death deities and reapers from all cultures congregated in the locker room. From the winged Valkyries to the demonesque Shinigami — speaking of, Todd stood in front of Grimm's locker, nervously fiddling with the ties of his robe. His crimson horns poked through his black hair, and his skin was a marbled swirl of grey.

"Oh, hey, Grimm. I was just wondering…" He trailed off under Grimm's eyeless stare but took a steadying breath and continued. "You skeleton types always creep me out. Anyway, I was wondering. Your record for making no mistakes and giving no second chances is legendary. I wanted to ask, since you are the best… Is there a good way to tell if a human is dead? I mean, an early reaping is not as bad as when Gerl swung her scythe backwards and accidentally revived Elvis, but I cannot afford another failure…"

Grimm ignored Todd's endless chatter and retrieved his robe and scythe before heading out the door.

"Hey! I was talking to y…" Todd's voice trailed off as Grimm entered his designated portal.

Grimm revelled in the quietness of death. Humans were so often silent from shock, or cried quietly, too afraid to speak. He didn't have to talk to anyone, and nobody bothered him with pointless conversation.

Grimm looked at the first entry on his list.

Maisy Winters, 87. Died in her sleep – Confirmed.

Her soul stood with her hands on the shoulders of her sobbing children, still tethered to her corpse by the silvery thread of fate. When she saw Grimm approach, she nodded sombrely at him. Grimm nodded back and swung his scythe, severing her soul from her body. He took her hand, and she followed him peacefully down the long, winding path through her memories, to the door to her afterlife.

The next three were also simple, confirmed deaths.

Alice Rhodes, 38. Drowned – Confirmed.

Peter Donaldson, 92. Heart attack – Confirmed.

Jim Andrews, 18. Avalanche while skiing – Confirmed.

Each reaping was different, but the long silent walk through the garden of memories was soothing for both the humans and Grimm. He saw all their greatest moments and biggest regrets. From first kisses to their final breath.

The last name on the list seemed like the others, but there was one slight difference.

Frank Jones, 26. Car crash victim – Needs Confirmation.

Grimm enjoyed these types of collections, where the opportunity to make the last call on their fatality rested with him. And apart from the occasional screamer, the shock kept them nice and quiet.

Frank's soul sat waiting on the bonnet of the smoking wreck that had been his car. As Grimm approached, Frank stood, nervously wiping his palms on his thighs.

"Oh, you must be Death. Ummm.... I think there has been a mistake. I'm not dead... okay, well, maybe a little dead. But I just need to not be dead for a little longer."

If Grimm had eyes, they would be rolling. He surveyed the scene; the body lay at an odd angle. It was clear Frank had not survived.

"What do you even do with our souls? Do you eat them? Ferry them to the afterlife? What is the afterlife like? Are there angels? Demons? Ghosts? No, wait, ghosts aren't in the afterlife, are they? Oh, are ghosts people that died when you were on holiday or something?"

Grimm gave the human his fiercest glare, but he continued to talk, completely unfazed.

"This might have been my fault; I was talking on the phone... My Da always said talking would be the death of me. Well, actually, he said, 'If you don't shut up, I'll kill ya myself!' which is basically the same thing."

Grimm felt a sense of horror creeping over him; this human would probably talk his way through the entire trip down memory lane.

"My boss gave me a raise last week. I didn't even ask for one. But he told me, 'If you stop coming in here and asking me questions all the bloody time, I'll give you a raise!' Can you believe it? So now I have to email him all my questions instead..."

Grimm could feel the rage radiating from himself as he raised his hand to interrupt. The human barrelled on, oblivious.

"I've always been a nervous talker, well, for the last 24 years at least. I don't think I talked much the first couple of years. I was actually on my way to see someone about it when I.... Yeah, well, there's this girl. I don't want to scare her away with my endless chatter. Though, I guess now, I'll scare no one away with my non-stop commentary. Well, it's not really a commentary, so much, more a stream of verbalised thoughts. Ma used to call it word vomit. I even do it when I'm alone. It's kind of my thing."

The only memories Frank would have were twenty-four years of constant talking.

Grimm prided himself on his professionalism, but the thought of all that talking sent shivers down his spine. He glanced at his list. Those two little words 'Needs Confirmation' stared back at him.

Frank opened his mouth again, no doubt to spew more banal chatter. Grimm couldn't take another word; he deftly swung his scythe in reverse. The silence washed over him as he walked away from the now miraculous, non-fatal crash.

Nobody talks to the Grimm Reaper, and that's how he prefers it.

The Rookery

Sarah Turner

George had been born here, had been vague and new here. He had pushed his pudgy hands across the chessboard tiles of the hall and closed his lids to ceilings adorned with medallions. As he grew, doors opened without argument, the old window in the morning room held on the first latch so that a small breeze rippled the nets, and whenever he returned from a trip, the house swelled around him, buoyed by his presence. But it never warmed to me.

I sat on the wide sill of the bay window, watching rain patter on the glass. He had been away for two months now, and I was aware of the whole house around me, of the empty space lingering at every doorway, spreading across the walnut floors. I felt the fireplace at my side, its tiles of mussel-shell blue, and beyond it, the dining room with its yawning table and snuffed-out chandeliers.

***

"Do you recognise the plates?"

George's face had glowed gold in the candlelight. The rest of the house sat in darkness, and I could almost hear the rooms closing up, folding away to nothing.

"Recognise them?" he said, glancing down.

"Yes."

He shrugged, apologetic.

"They're a wedding gift."

He smiled, eyes shining. "Ah, of course."

Silver clinked on china.

"I need you to know I'm heading to the recruiting office tomorrow morning."

I looked at my plate, at the flowers revealing themselves beneath the gravy. "Please, George."

"This isn't a choice, it's duty. What would I do if I stayed here?"

"Be with me," I said as crocuses and snowdrops bloomed.

"Darling, you know I can't."

"But what if—"

"I'm sorry."

I looked up. His taut features softened in the heat from the flames, and I thought that if I touched his cheek, my finger would leave its ridged print on his skin.

"I'll get the coffee," I said, moving away into the corridor, my footsteps summoning the other rooms into being.

***

When the rain broke, I took my coat from the little porch; its lifeless, blue body huddled next to Georges' grey one. The sandy path stretched away from me, winding through a sea of grass before sloping down to ancient elms where rooks nested and cried out through the night. Sometimes I lay awake and listened to them, finding solace in their aching voices as they hung unanswered in the air. I heard them the day of our wedding, in the beech trees that huddled round the church. I'd thought them bad luck, but George said they brought good fortune, and it was only when they abandoned the rookery that there was something to fear. He told me a group of them was known as a 'parliament', and we had laughed at the thought of them perched on branches, debating how rook society should be run.

I stepped off the path and walked in the other direction towards a rougher patch of land where we'd planted carrots, potatoes and onions. Their sharp scent filled the warm air as they ripened, moons waiting to be pulled from the earth. When I stood here, it was okay to mourn his absence, to plant my feet in the recently disturbed soil and let tears run down my face. I could tell myself it was only the onions.

That night, fires rekindled after I beat them out, and doors creaked ajar after their handles were twisted shut.

"It's not my fault," I said, my small voice drifting through the rooms and up the coiling staircase. "I tried to get him to stay."

With only the light of a candle, the bedroom walls—by day a soft blue—became a washed-out grey, and the coiffed figures who rode horses and lounged against trees had disappeared entirely, had ridden deep into the walls and found shelter in distant cottages. I was truly alone.

I rested my arms on the sill and looked out into the garden: darkness had taken the vegetable patch and the small iron table, but I knew if I were to walk down there, it would give them back to me. A buck moon, full and yellow, rose behind the trees, and as I stared, I remembered it was its own thing, distant and orbiting, not some decoration hammered into the ceiling of sky. And there were other things too, weren't there? Beyond the trees was a butcher's and a grocer's and a shop that sold hats and strings of pearls; beyond that, the sea, forever braving the French coast then running away again; and beyond that, the cities and the mud and the bands of men.

    A lone rook cawed, both mournful and pathetic, and I felt my usual pang of sympathy. Another called out, louder and fiercer, and again I sympathised. Then a whole chorus began, screeching and chaotic, a parliament of yelling suits and calls for order. Fear shot through me. There was a rushing, swooping sound as they flew from the trees, hundreds of them jet black against the moon, leaving behind tangled nests and bad fortune.

    "Come back!" I called as their shapes shrank to nothing. "Come back!"

    My hand burned on the banister as I hurried down the stairs. When I reached the hall, the front door was already open. Grey light crept over the threshold, reaching out to glass tables, silvered mirrors and clock faces that read midnight. The doors to the other rooms were still shut, but when the wind blew, their handles rattled, urgent and determined. I grabbed my coat from the rack, draped it around my shoulders and ran into the garden.

    The trees were quiet as I approached, but I didn't stop until I was under their dark canopies, the empty rookery above me. They weren't coming back.

"They never migrate," George had said, his own hair rook-like with its black sheen. "Some do, further north, but not these."

We had sat here only a few months ago, a gingham blanket rolled out beneath us, the spring sun at our backs. George spoke of the war then, but it didn't seem real when surrounded by flasks of tea and plates of sandwiches and the house looking like a wedding cake, its white front piped and glistening.

"Tell me more about the rooks," I had said, leaning back on my elbows, listening to the soft beat of wings.

Now, the house was a ghost, bright and strange in the moonlight, and I imagined it unlatching at the side, its grand facade arcing across the path, its space neatly divided into rooms full of dressers and desks and lamps that were cold to the touch. George was moving between the rooms, passing through doorways to the parlour, the dining room, the kitchen, the hall—his tall figure forever wandering. I shut my eyes for a moment, breathed in the night air, then took small steps back up the path.

The lion's head gleamed; the hinge clamped between its sharp teeth like prey. Risking a bite, I rapped it against the plate. No answer. The house had shut me out. I sank down, my back against the heavy door, the arched portico above me. A dull grey was creeping onto the horizon, and I watched with no awareness of time as lilac streaked and the sun spilled over the trees. George once told me his favourite time of day was early morning because everything flared like struck matches, and I imagined the house at my back, its windows full of fire and rage.

"Ma'am?"

I blinked my eyes open. The sky was bright blue, and the sun was high. I must have fallen asleep.

"Ma'am?"

A boy stood before me—he couldn't have been older than fifteen. He was dressed head to foot in khaki green, and a belt was clasped at his waist. In his hand was a brown envelope. I stood up.

"I have a telegram for a Mrs Braddock."

"I'm Mrs Braddock," I said, holding out a hand and smoothing my coat with the other.

He squinted as if trying to see me better, then handed over the letter.

I ran my fingers across the scrawled address, smudging the pencil. I considered leaving it unopened, propping it up on one of the tables to sit and gather dust, its words unread and unrealised. But that wouldn't do. I watched the boy until he disappeared round the bend of the drive, then ripped at the seal.

They regretted to inform me.

The sun burned at the back of my neck, and small birds chirped and whistled.

They regretted to inform me.

There were the sounds of car horns from the town, of horse hooves and feet on paving slabs.

They regretted to inform me.

I beat my fists on the door until my knuckles hurt, then slumped my weight against it, hands over my face to block out the sun and its garish, thoughtless light.

"Please," I whispered, although to whom I wasn't sure.

There was a clicking sound, a familiar twist of metal; the door opened, and the house embraced me.

The Neighborhood

Kerr Pelto

Shurlene tied a stained apron around her waist and started working on Doris. Though she couldn't make herself look beautiful, no matter how much makeup she applied, Shurlene was a natural at beautifying her customers. She'd pretend they were family. Doris could be a long-lost aunt; she looked like she would have been sweet, like she'd swing her front door wide open when Shurlene pulled into the driveway. Like she'd have homemade cookies warming in the oven and sweetened iced tea on the table. Like they'd talk for hours about their day. Doris would hug and kiss Shurlene goodbye and tell her she couldn't wait to see her next Friday, same time. Shurlene wished Doris lived in her neighborhood. They would have been great friends. But it wouldn't work. She didn't know Doris.

Her boss, owner of Ashes to Ashes Crematorium, approached her from behind like a spider. His voice, sandpapered by decades of smoking, rasped, "What's taking you so long? She's dead. She doesn't have to win a beauty contest. And George needs cooking before your shift ends."

Like Jekyll and Hyde, her money-grubbing boss would be all smiles and condolences to the bereaved in the foyer, but his feigned sensitivity stopped there. He detested the cold bodies of their loved ones.

Shurlene's compassion for the forgotten, those without family, consumed her waking hours as well as her fantasies. As if the small amount of love she gave them would cover up all their scars.

Shurlene found George, naked on the sliding table jutting out of the incinerator. She took off his wedding ring and pocketed it, feeling it had surely meant something to him. Before she slid him in, she nodded her head in prayer and waved her hand over him like a benediction. She wanted all who left this earth to find peace elsewhere. To find a heavenly family. Well, maybe not all. Maybe not Ms. Elizabeth.

After incinerating George and two other forgotten souls, Shurlene snatched twenty bucks from Mr. Grimes' desk and drove back to her neighborhood, to the houses filled with those she loved.

***

In the morning, Shurlene donned her threadbare uniform and drove her Ford Pinto to her morning job at Sunset Hills. The rundown buildings would have glowed with the rising sun, but decades of neglect marred their stone façades. Shurlene walked through the double doors and signed in. She acknowledged the receptionist.

"Mabel."

"Shurlene. You're late. Again."

"Pinto. Acting up."

"Right." Mabel shook her head at the overused excuse.

Shurlene tucked her chin to her flat chest and hobbled down the hall to Room 4. The stench of soiled sheets and Emma's unwashed body singed the hairs in Shurlene's pockmarked nose.

"Ms. Ward, I'm gonna take good care of you. Let's get you into the shower, change your clothes, and you can sit in the recliner while I change your sheets."

"My sweet Charlene, you're the only one who cares for me in this dump."

Shurlene never corrected Ms. Ward. Did a name really matter? Hers didn't. Not even to her mother. That's why she loved her neighborhood and considered everyone in those houses as family.

Shurlene lathered Emma's hair with baby shampoo until it was squeaky clean. Emma sat in her recliner while Shurlene combed through her wet hair, carefully styling the white curls to frame her petite, wrinkled face. "Ms. Emma, I've been caring for you well over a year now. Are you my friend?"

"Of course I am, Charlene. I've told you many times I'd be your friend, forever."

"Wouldn't it be even better if we were family, Ms. Emma?"

"Do you not have a family? Where's your momma? Your daddy? Don't you have any brothers or sisters?"

"They're all dead, Ms. Emma."

"I'm so sorry to hear that, child. If you want me to be family, it's okay with me."

"I wish *you* had been my mother. Mine was cruel to me."

"Well, that settles it, deary. You've been a better daughter to me than my narcissistic, good-for-nothing Darlene. She thinks I'm dead already."

That last statement gave Shurlene hope. She smiled as she put fresh sheets on the bed, opened the window to let in some fresh air, then turned on the TV to the Hallmark channel. "I'll come back at lunchtime to wheel you to the cafeteria. We're having meatloaf today."

"That slice of cardboard!?"

Shurlene burst out laughing. She left to tend to her next resident and lowered her head as she walked by Mabel who was stuffing her mouth with a greasy hamburger.

"Did you take care of that old cow? She wouldn't stop buzzing me this morning."

Shurlene mumbled to the floor, "Wish you'd croak."

"What did you say?"

"Um, wish I had a Coke."

"Well, you know where they are. I'm not getting you one."

Of course you aren't. You can't get up from your chair. You're wedged into it. You never do anything for me. All you do is make fun and tell me I'm worthless. You wouldn't even take care of sweet Ms. Ward.

Shurlene limped into Room 17. She fingered the cross dangling from her neck and eyed Ms. Elizabeth's jewelry piled on top of the dresser.

"Morning, Shirley."

"Name's Shurlene."

"Shurlene. Shirley. Makes no difference to me."

Ms. Elizabeth coughed until Shurlene thought the old crone's lungs would explode. Pointing to Shurlene's platform shoe, she said, "How much shorter is your left leg?"

"Two inches."

"What happened?"

"I was born."

The old hag snickered. "Hmmm. Short leg. Hooked nose. Limp brown hair. And cross-eyed to boot. Betcha no man has ever kept your bed warm." Ms. Elizabeth scooted her obese hips to the side of the bed. "About time you got here. Help me to the toilet."

Shurlene did as she was told and closed the bathroom door. After she dispensed a dose of arsenic into Ms. Elizabeth's orange juice, she snatched the diamond earrings from off the dresser. She'd hock them and use the cash to buy something for her neighborhood. Maybe a new tree.

She helped Ms. Elizabeth back into the same stale sheets and said, "I'll see you tomorrow morning, Ms. Elizabeth." *If you don't die first.*

Shurlene finished her morning rounds, then took her bagged lunch into Ms. Ward's room. "Ms. Emma, I made an extra pastrami and ham on rye today if you'd like it. I know you hate the meatloaf." Shurlene sat beside Ms. Emma, dug her hand into the well-used paper bag, and brought out two limp sandwiches.

Emma opened the drawer to the bedside table and pulled out her stash of vodka. Shurlene never could figure out how Emma got the liquor, but she knew why. The staff wouldn't know the difference between the clear alcohol and water. Emma had been drinking her 'water' for months, and Shurlene wasn't about to tattle on her.

Mabel stopped Shurlene before she left for the day. "I'd say 'Have a nice evening,' but I doubt you will."

***

Once home, Shurlene needed to unload her negative emotions onto her neighborhood friends, the ones she considered family. First, she talked to Inez in the blue house. She told Inez all about how horrid Ms. Elizabeth was. Then she practiced her French with Claudette, who was in the green house. Shurlene's accent wasn't perfect, but Claudette didn't mind, wouldn't say a word while Shurlene expounded on Mabel's bullying and Mr. Grimes' neglect. Next was Isabelle. The pink house. Shurlene knew Isabelle loved pink, so why wouldn't she get to have a pink one? Shurlene told Isabelle about her visit with Ms. Emma. How blind Ms. Emma always made her feel loved. Always couldn't wait to see her every day. Ms. Emma would hold her hands in her own frail ones, saying how soft Shurlene's hands were. Shurlene told all her neighbors she thought a newcomer might be joining them soon.

***

Shurlene woke up the next day with a queasy feeling in the pit of her stomach and rushed to Sunset Hills. She walked lopsidedly down the hall to Emma's Room. The bed was stripped, empty. Shurlene opened the drawer to the bedside table. Wrapped around the bottle of vodka with a rubber band was a note. In an elegant though wobbly scrawl, it said, "For Shurlene, the beautiful, kindhearted daughter I wish I'd had. Love, Emma, a.k.a. Mom."

Love? No one had ever said that to Shurlene. She sat on the bed for the next half hour, unable to move, tears streaming down her face, uncontrolled, smudging her meticulous attempt at masking her face with cheap makeup.

Mabel waddled into the room. "Done crying like a baby? You gotta leave. Housekeeping needs to come in, disinfect, and make the bed. We have a real winner moving in this afternoon."

"When did Ms. Emma die? Why didn't you call me?"

"During the night, obviously. Why call? Who cares?"

Shurlene jumped off the bed and faced Mabel. In a disturbingly quiet voice, she said, "I care, Mabel. She's family."

"She ain't your family. You're as pathetic as your face and bum leg."

"Where's Emma?!"

"At Ashes to Ashes, shit-for-brains. It's the only funeral home in town."

Shurlene pushed past Mabel. On her way out, she dumped MiraLAX into Mabel's Diet Coke.

At Ashes to Ashes, she flung the back door open and rushed to the cold bins that held bodies for cremation.

"What're you doing here?"

"Boss! Where's Ms. Ward?"

"She's in the incinerator. Ten more minutes. Why all the tears?"

"She's my moth ... I cared for her at Sunset Hills. She was fine yesterday."

"She wasn't fine this morning when they found her on the floor."

"Anyone asking for her ashes?"

"Nope."

The doorbell clanged. Mr. Grimes yanked off his gloves and white lab coat, then put on his low-budget suit jacket. As he headed out the door to greet new clients, he said, "You might as well finish up with Ms. Ward."

Shurlene sat in the back room and sobbed over the loss of her friend, the one she called Mother, the only person in the world who showed her any love.

The buzzer sounded, notifying Shurlene the cremation chamber had completed its work. Gathering the remains, she ground them to ashes, her tears soaking into the mix. She picked up the urn with Emma's name on it and poured into it all that was left of her friend. Well, almost all. She grabbed her prescription bottle of Caplyta inside her purse, emptied the contents back into her bag, and replaced them with Emma's ashes. She found a manila folder with Emma's name on it, opened it, and found the only piece of jewelry she'd ever worn. A ring. A family heirloom. She put it on her finger and left.

***

Back home, Shurlene sat in her tattered armchair and admired her neighborhood. The warm rays of the sun penetrated her dingy window and landed on all the little houses meticulously arranged on her thrift store table. She picked up the miniature ceramic house she bought for Emma at Goodwill. There had been so many reasons to choose white. It made her think of purity and peacefulness. Angels, even. Everything the kind, old woman had been to her.

Turning the tiny house over, she uncorked the bottom and poured Emma inside. The little house took its place of honor between Inez and Isabelle. Claudette wouldn't mind; wouldn't say a word.

The ring on Shurlene's finger sparkled as she raised the flask of vodka to her lips. "You're family now, Momma. Welcome to my neighborhood."

Stretched

James Hancock

Doc Dianne's chat show was all the rage ten years ago, but like most things, she became old and stale. Her prime time slot moved further into the obscure hours and her guests were C-listers at best. Ted watches through sleepy eyes as Doc Dianne explains the miracle of childbirth to three pregnant nobodies. He watches and wonders what authority she has on the subject: leathery smoker's skin, hairy upper lip, in her seventies, never married, and no kids. How much are her guests being paid to smile and nod along? Bobble heads. Ted is a lazy researcher, but if needs must, he can do better than this.

Click! The TV turns off.

Facing the screen is Ted. Wild-haired, unshaven, and the wrong end of forty. He sits in a worn, bolognaise-stained armchair, wearing off-white Y-fronts and balancing a plate of chocolate cake on a round belly. He drops the TV controller onto a grubby cream carpet, slides a slice of cake from the plate and stuffs it into his mouth. Crumbs fall, clinging to chin whiskers and chest hair.

Ted finger hooks chocolate icing from his bellybutton, adds it to the overload of brown muck he is working on and stands up. The plate of cake is carelessly discarded onto the armchair, and he walks across the drab and untidy living room of a carefree bachelor. A slob. He supports his belly with both hands. A pale and chocolate crumb speckled belly, covered in a wiry black fuzz of hair, and considerably larger than it should be compared to the rest of Ted's frame.

He waddles out of the room, tears rolling down his cheeks. Once again, he is the victim of unexplainable emotions. This is not a midlife crisis. This is not just a man who has given up and let neglect rot in. This is something entirely different.

Overly tired, and still chomping cake, Ted takes his belly to bed. The end of a typical evening.

***

Ted begins his morning ritual in the same way he has the last few months. Head in toilet and violently heaving up last night's junk food. Brush teeth. More vomit, and then stroking his balloon belly. He admires his side profile; running his hands over angry pink stretch marks. She's a beauty.

None of Ted's clothes fit properly, and everything is uncomfortable now. Tracksuit again; the same as yesterday. He checks his phone, grabs his keys and the pregnancy test, and leaves his flat. This is it. If doctor Patel won't listen, Ted knows what he must do. Keep calm and carry on. There's always his best friend, Ollie. Ollie will be the rock he needs if all else fails.

***

Doctor Patel's office is much like any other. Chunky desk with monitor supposedly showing Ted's notes, if he cared to look and attempt translation. A bed covered with blue paper towel sheets. And other things which would be easily forgotten should they ever be acknowledged in the first place. Ted stares at the pregnancy test on the desk. Positive.

Doctor Patel holds up a medical book showing the female anatomy. Womb, ovaries... Doctor Patel's lips are moving, but Ted can't take it in. He is distracted by movement and pressure against his bladder. There's every chance a memorable addition to the office decor is minutes away. He fidgets, manoeuvring his sweaty and partially numb rump over the hard blue fabric of the patient's chair. Why is everything blue, white, or grey in here?

Still holding the book for Ted to see, Doctor Patel points at a detailed pencil drawing of a woman's body, shaking his head and emphasising something with a waving of his hand. More grey on white. Ted wants to grab the book and ram it up Doctor Patel's arse.

Doctor Patel puts the book aside and continues his speech as he picks up the pregnancy test. He shakes his head some more and makes a definite 'no' hand motion.

Ted blurts a forceful yawp. The death gurgle of a frustrated camel: long, loud, and directly at Doctor Patel. Doctor Patel stops talking, stunned by the sudden interruption.

Ted gets up, pushes a palm against his semi numb and painful lower back, pulls the pregnancy test from Doctor Patel's hand, and walks out of his office. Doctor Patel sees Ted's camel impression and matches it with wide-eyed fish.

***

With the big day drawing ever closer, Ted stares at his prepared goods whilst munching from a jar of pickled gherkins: maternity clothes, sanitary towels, Vaseline, baby formula, nappies, and a bottle of whisky in case things become too painful. He's not sure what to expect, but thanks to Ollie's last-minute work trip out of the country and Doctor Patel's closed-mindedness, Ted knows he'll be going it alone.

If Ollie were here, he'd... he'd remind Ted of his blasphemous remark about Mary and the virgin birth. He'd remind him that some comments are heard and get a reply. Ted realises the probability he has pissed off God. Shit! No, this isn't some kind of twisted punishment. This is a miracle. A blessing. This is his destiny. The fates came together and chose him from billions of candidates. He's special.

A painful kick to the lower abdomen pushes thoughts of 'why' to one side and turns Ted's concentration to 'how'. How he is going to deliver said predicament into the world.

He considers the limited options for an exit point and pours himself a large whisky.

***

Screams carry through the night. Ted is propped up on his bed with the help of half a dozen pillows, dressing gown open and legs spread wide. Sweat pours, tears flow, Vaseline is generously applied, and whisky is drunk. Ted's thoughts are brief and dashed with each overriding surge of agony. Are there special breathing methods? He should have bought a tens machine. There's not going to be enough whisky. How the fuck do women do this? Arghhhhhhh!

Three long and excruciating hours of blood, sweat and a brown jelly substance later, Ted pulls something free and lifts it from the swampy sheets. An egg. Ted has given birth to an egg the size of a honeydew melon. Exhausted, he pops it on his chest and laughs hysterically. The laughter turns to tears. The ordeal is over.

**

Ted considers the likelihood he'll never walk the same way again. Certain parts of the body shouldn't be stretched to such a size, and all prayers of having it snap back into shape have fallen unanswered. Four sanitary pads jammed between his cheeks and held in with elasticated maternity knickers. The only comfortable garment is a flowery dress he picked up from a charity shop for a fiver. Bargain! A little tight around the waist, but he is carrying post-egg belly.

He waddles through the park with his legs wide apart and an arsehole that feels, and probably looks should he ever brave it, like a burst balloon. The healing process is going to be long and uncomfortable. He makes a mental note to add more E45 cream to his next shop. And more whisky.

He gets funny looks from those walking past, but he smiles in return, whistling a jaunty tune as he pushes Shelly along in a pram. The proud father.

In the movies, people stop and admire the baby. Ted has encountered no such people.

***

Shelly's corner of the bedroom is decorated with animal stickers on the wall, cuddly toys, and a fluffy clouds mobile hanging over a Moses basket. More charity shop bargains. The egg rests inside the basket, atop a baby blanket, wrapped in a nappy, and doing very little. As expected.

Ted rolls his fingers and makes peekaboo noises. Disappearing and reappearing for the amusement of his egg. He stops and frowns. He stares at the egg, waiting for something. Anything. The egg... the egg does nothing.

Ted had heard wondrous things about the joys of parenthood, mostly from Doc Dianne, but he wasn't getting anything from it. Apart from the seeping, an angry rash, and difficulty in sitting, things are mostly how they were before. There is no inner glow. There is no strong bond. Doc Dianne is full of shit.

Shelly needs a personality. Something Ted can attach to. He raids his pens and crayons tin, digs out a sharpie, and goes to work. Two big black circle eyes and a smiley mouth above the nappy's waistband. Humpty Dumpty comes to mind, but it's better than nothing.

***

Ted sits uncomfortably on a cushion in his kitchen doorway. He laughs theatrically and makes several whooshing noises as he gives Shelly a little bounce in a baby doorway bouncer. He remembers his mother's photo album and seeing the smile on his face as he sat in his doorway bouncer. As far as thrills go, this is the baby equivalent of bungee jumping and a rollercoaster all in one. The best of the best.

He bounces his egg with a little more gusto in the hopes of a response, but nothing. He pulls the bouncer low and twangs high with an excitable whee! The egg comes loose and gives flight. Ted's beaming smile drops and he gawps in bewilderment as he watches Shelly, catapulted at the optimal angle, slow-motion overhead and across the living room. Crack!

Ted rushes to Shelly, lifts the egg in his arms, and thick yolk oozes over the living room carpet. Long slippery dollops slide through his fingers. Failing to keep hold of Shelly's juices, he falls to his knees, screaming. Why? Why wasn't he more careful? Why didn't... he stops and looks at his yolk-coated hands. Lost in thought for a moment, he wipes a sleeve across his tears and allows himself a brief nod of inner agreement.

***

Ted sits in his armchair, watching Doc Dianne share her pearls of wisdom with an audience of middle-aged nodding heads. Once again, he relaxes in his off-white Y-fronts and ketchup-stained dressing gown. Atop his pale fuzzy belly rests a plate filled with a mountain of steaming hot scrambled egg.

Ted slaps the bottom of a ketchup bottle, spilling a generous dollop over the egg. He shovels a fork in and eats.

A Family's Honor

Christopher Bloodworth

"God-fuckin' damn it! Shee-it!"

The blasphemous words, in all their profane glory, exploded through the woods like a firework for all the neighboring campers to hear. Gary winced and looked apologetically at his wife, Jen.

"You should say something to them, Gary."

Gary looked doubtfully at the camp a dozen yards away. Evidently, the man who had shouted the string of curses had sliced a finger while trying to open what must have been his twelfth beer by using one hand to wedge the edge of the bottle cap against the bark of a tree and then slamming his other hand down on top of the bottle to pry the cap. Gary recognized the brand of beer and rolled his eyes. It was a twist cap. The other man was still laughing drunkenly at his injured friend.

"Please, Gary? Just go talk to them. For heaven's sake, our *kids* are here."

Gary groaned inwardly. Jen was a wonderful woman, but she was... sensitive. And if she confessed that her plan for educating their two children on the birds and bees was to hand over a letter on their respective wedding nights—a tasteful letter touching upon just the essentials of the business—suffice it to say, Gary would not be surprised. As for strong language, if Jen had her way, the children of the world would live and die without ever hearing so much as a "piss" or a "crap", let alone a "fuck" or a "sheeit."

"I... could talk to them I guess," he mumbled.

"Well, get over there then."

"Ok, ok, I'm... I'll..."

But Gary didn't know what he would do. He tried thinking of something to say, but the harder he thought, the blanker his mind became. Propelled by the eyes of his wife, he was standing, then walking, then—to his horror—found himself a mere arm's length from these men who had fallen into perplexed silence at his awkward approach.

"... Can we help you, sir?"

"Hi, yes. How are you?"

They nodded.

"Good. Yes, well... You see, we... We wondered—well, my wife, she wondered. See, our kids are here, for a little family vacation, and we—my wife—she, she wanted to see if you could maybe keep some of the spicier profanity down. A bit. For...for the kids, you know. And... for my wife..."

The drunken cussers looked amusedly at each other, and the man who had cut his thumb replied to Gary with mock sincerity.

"Yessir, we hear ya. We'll keep it down—Scout's honor. Y'all enjoy your vacation now."

"Wow, we really appreciate it, fellas! Thanks, and sorry for the bother." With a diminutive bow of the head, Gary turned back towards his family. He knew his performance had lacked... finesse. But despite their mockery, Gary believed the men would keep their word, and he felt a deep pride in his accomplishment. Unfortunately, the injured cusser didn't trouble to keep his voice quite low enough as Gary walked away.

"Shit, if his wife wanted us to pipe down so bad, maybe the bitch shoulda come over to tell us herself."

Gary froze, face rigid, ears hot with the men's laughter. He'd barely registered that he was back at his family's tent until his wife interrupted his thoughts.

"Hey, how'd it go?"

"Hmm? Oh," he said, coming back to himself, "they said they'd keep it down."

"Really?"

"Yep."

"Well, thanks for doing that. I'm proud of you for standing up to them".

"Yeah... no problem."

But it was a problem. It was a *big* problem. 'Thanks for standing up to them?' He hadn't stood up to them. But he would. By God, before the day was out, he would.

"Hey, Jen? Any leftover coffee from this morning?"

"It's in the van." She raised an eyebrow. "Pretty late for coffee though. Dinner's in an hour. Won't it keep you up?"

"Well, I think I just need a pick-me-up. Might even make a bit more."

Thermos in hand, Gary stared at the cusser camp with blazing intensity, keeping eye contact even when he tilted his head back to drink the warm coffee, which he swigged with the vigor and purpose of an alcoholic.

As Gary drank his coffee, the cussers drank through their stockpile of beers until, running out, they opened the bourbon. Gary smiled.

"Honey?" His brain vaguely registered that Jen was speaking to him. "It's time for bed."

"You go ahead. Guess you were right about the coffee," he smiled, shrugging apologetically. "Can't sleep."

She rolled her eyes but smiled back and whispered goodnight as she zipped herself into the tent. He was alone. The time had come.

Rising, Gary walked to the cusser's camp, unzipped their tent, and entered. There they both lay, their filthy mouths agape in drunkenness. Gary smiled as he felt the coffee roiling through him, shaking his bowels. Quietly, he moved to a squatting position, pulling his pants to his ankles. Holding one hand behind him to catch the deposits, Gary concentrated on pushing. He needed only two—a "shee-it" apiece for each foul mouth whose tongues were unworthy to even say his wife's name.

One.

Two.

Gary gently placed his shit into their open mouths, pushing until their gag reflexes were activated. Yet through gurgles and chokes, neither man awoke from his drunken sleep. But in a few hours, they would. Would they understand when they did? Would they change their ways? No. And that was ok. Gary wasn't here to teach lessons.

As Gary wiped up, his face twisted in disgust at the sound of smacking—the man who'd called Jen "bitch" had worked the shit up from the back of his throat and now was gnawing at it like a cow chewing cud. He knew he would need to move his family at first light, and they would want to know why. But he didn't need to worry about that right now. Leaving the spluttering men behind, Gary departed for his own camp knowing he could rest for a few hours, satisfied in a job well done, his family's honor defended.

The Lost Temple of Osiris

Ryan Fleming

Not all secrets are meant to be uncovered. There are certain truths that must remain shrouded in mystery, beyond the reach of humanity's understanding. Alas, I wasn't privy to this wisdom, and now, in my plagued existence, pen these words as a warning. Let these scrawls serve as a deterrent to any who dare delve into the cursed mysteries of the lost Temple of Osiris. My shattered mind strains under the weight of this curse, and the sweet release of oblivion is all I crave. In my trembling hand rests the instrument of my escape.

Legends state the temple was buried deep in the Egyptian sands, hidden by the gods. Remnants of faded, cryptic hieroglyphs bear the arcane message: *It sees.*

Countless seekers have attempted to locate the lost Temple of Osiris, only to fail. But fortune favored me, for my team stumbled upon a macabre artifact, an Egyptian tablet depicting the vile Osiris devouring a human offering. This revelation would have brought me fame, but a thirst for greater discovery consumed me.

Deciphering the possible location from the runes on the tablet, I assembled a crew of five brave souls and set out into the arid desert. With the artifact as our guide, we sought to uncover the only entrance to the buried temple. Using the stars on the tablet in conjunction with those in the sky, we resolved to tunnel beneath the shifting sands toward a narrow aperture we believed was the key to entering Osiris's sanctum.

I loathe to confess, as I drove my shovel into that first dune, a nameless terror gripped me - a feeling of being watched by unseen entities. The most mundane of objects, a compass, a canteen cap, even my pocket watch, seemed to flicker with sinister animation in the corner of my vision. I tried to dispel these phantoms as mere illusions brought on by the heat, but to no avail.

We burrowed deeper into compressed sand, hardened through time, discovering a shaft that sloped down into uncharted depths. The terror grew stronger, infecting my mind and senses with every step. The shadows thrown by our torches, spaced every few feet, assumed monstrous shapes that mocked and tormented us. Even the glint of sand crystals in the darkness took on the appearance of baleful eyes, watching our every move.

Just before we broke through the subterranean chasm, our first companion snapped. He shrieked in frenzied terror, clapping his hands over his eyes and sprinting madly toward the surface. "It sees me!" he cried.

His words struck a chord of dread within me, and I saw fear ripple through the rest of my crew. I should have heeded this warning, but the lure of exploration held me in its thrall, stronger than my terror.

Despite the mounting apprehension, I ordered my team to press on, descending deeper into the unknown.

With one final blow of a pickaxe, our company broke into a Stygian blackness where the light of our torches could not penetrate. A noxious stench flooded the tunnel, inflaming our lungs. Wracked with uncontrollable coughing, two of my crew dared not advance any farther and retreated to the surface for respite.

The two men who remained with me trembled, imploring me to extinguish my torch, muttering, "It sees us!"

With the prospect of a phenomenal discovery, I summoned all my resolve and berated my companions for their cowardice. Alone, yet undaunted, I stepped forward into the maw of the dark cavern.

For but an instant, my torch flickered, illuminating my magnificent find. The walls were shaped like the pyramids of Giza, adorned with massive sculptures of great stone beasts offering allegiance to an immense idol that I immediately identified as Osiris. I had, at last, uncovered his fabled lost temple.

However, I was struck by a dreadful realization - did the statue of Osiris move? I dared to cast my light upwards, seeking to dispel my mounting fear, and met the unshakable sight of the deity's countenance directed toward me. His eyes, blazing with a fiery hue, pierced through the darkness, into my soul.

To have met an untimely end would be merciful compared to what I witnessed. Oh God! Nothing has allowed me to forget those seconds of my meager existence, for I cannot escape this obsessive curse! It was within that moment that the vile statue of the Egyptian god gave a single, deliberate blink and shifted its eyes to bear down upon me. The anguished cries of my comrades echoed throughout the temple's complex. Overcome by primal terror, I fled back to the tunnel. Disregarding the fate of my late companions, who now lay motionless on the ground, I raced to escape the accursed temple.

Panic-stricken, I ran up the treacherous sand shaft, my foot stumbling upon the lifeless forms of my hapless comrades, their heads forcibly buried in the walls of our man-made tunnel. The final crew member lay at its entrance, his eyes gouged out, and face contorted in a gruesome display of terror.

I emerged in the cold of a desert night, and grasping a shovel, feverishly attempted to seal the passage. My efforts were in vain as, without warning, the tunnel caved in on itself.

Collapsing, I gasped for air and gazed up at the full moon. Even its serene light offered no solace, for it blinked like a malevolent eye, glaring down upon me. Overcome with horror, I lost consciousness.

Though saved by desert nomads and taken far from that accursed place, a piece of me remains trapped in the desert, lost forever. I am tormented by the unblinking gaze of the thing that ceaselessly watches me. Its unwavering stare haunts my dreams, piercing through the veil of my attempts to ignore it. I cannot escape its constant vigil.

Even as I write this, that vicious eye watches! Watches, watches, always watches! I am held captive by that relentless gaze, tearing at my very soul. I must flee from this unyielding pursuit, for I can endure it no longer. I see no other end. There is only one thing left, to find freedom and be rid of this nightmare. The barrel of my revolver beckons.

The Final Confession

Jonathan Braunstein

Father Shannon stared into the cream that swirled about in his nominal coffee at Hedge's, the local diner, questioning his decision to accept the assignment of the Smithtown Parish. The residents of this quaint Oklahoma town were kind enough, but there was no openness to attending Sunday morning masses. Sometimes a friendly skirting of the invite, but more often than not, they were members of the large Evangelical Church just outside of town. Perhaps it was time to leave this place as there was clearly no need for what the Catholic Church could offer. Each week he saw a few backsliders who decided to give his church a try. Except for Mrs. Greenwich, an elderly congregant, who never missed Mass but for this past week.

He loosened his clerical collar and typed on his smartphone, contact Mrs. G. He then began to pen the words of his resignation. In his peripheral, he saw a large hand extend to him.

"I sincerely apologize for not welcomin' you to the area. The ministry is... well you know how it is." A hulking figure of a man flashed pearly white teeth in an overly welcoming smile while his hand waited.

Father Shannon placed his phone down. He instinctively paused before taking the proffered hand, noticing the man's thick, yellowed nails, he gripped firmly. "Reverend Blake of Pleasant Gorge Evangelical. I've heard a lot of great things."

"Believe none of it," Reverend Blake said with a chuckle as he sat across in the booth without an invite. "More than half of what is attributed to us men of the cloth is perception anyhow."

Whether or not he agreed, Shannon brightened by the refreshing directness. "My hope is... I mostly stay true to myself."

Blake reached across the table and placed his meaty hand on Father Shannon's shoulder and kept it there. For a moment, the plastic smile dropped from his face, replaced with a dour, grim look. "I agree whole-heartedly. Full disclosure, that's why I'm here. I need to talk with a man like you."

"Do you mean to confess? It's not usually done in a public place like this. Perhaps we can arrange a time, meet at the confessional and—"

"No," the reverend said, shaking his head. He removed his hand from Shannon's shoulder and softened his countenance. "My congregation knows nothing of it. I've been hiding it best I can, but I fear I can no longer. Time isn't on my side, friend."

Father Shannon's heart quickened with compassion. "How long do you have?"

The reverend whispered, "I risked even saying it to you here. I haven't seen a doctor. Even if he remains quiet, his staff would talk." He eyed the room for any prying ears.

"I've studied and know the signs. I have a few days at most."

Not knowing what to say, Father Shannon uttered, "I'm so sorry."

With a sincere, weak smile, Blake asked, "Can we meet in my home? Where I'm... comfortable?"

"By all means, I'll just pay for my coffee, and we can go right away."

Blake placed his hand over the bill. "I got it. It's the least I can do." His left eye twitched as he grinned. He took hold of the check and slipped it into his sport coat's pocket and made his way to the register at the counter.

Reverend Blake poured on the charm with the aging waitress, complimenting her outfit and red curly hair.

She responded in kind and even blushed from the momentary, boisterous attention. "Why both you men of God can just have it on the house," she said with glee, playfully slapping his arm.

Shannon thought Reverend Blake's schmoozing ways might be what was needed to make headway in this town. He felt justified in leaving. His resignation would have to wait. This morning, he hoped to alleviate the conscience of a dying man of God. He reached down for his phone, but it was no longer there. Did Reverend Blake pick it up by accident, thinking it was his? As he walked to the register, he asked, "Do you—"

"I don't mind driving. I'm parked out back." In quick fashion, he brushed past Father Shannon and headed out the rear hallway.

"That's not what I was going to ask at all," Shannon said to himself, not realizing he said it loud enough for the waitress to hear, who shrugged in response.

Shannon walked toward the hallway that led out the back.

As he passed the last booth, a drunk man clutched his sleeve. "Don't go, Father," he said. His eyes bloodshot and breath wreaking of whisky and burnt coffee. "That man of God is no good." He continued to froth and babble incoherently, 'fresh' or 'flesh' being the only word Shannon could decipher.

The father patted the drunk man's bony hand. "I don't let a difference of opinion concerning communion bother me and neither should you. You walk home and get some rest." As he attempted to leave, the drunk man gripped Shannon's arm but the man's hand fell limp and he let go.

Walking through the heavy, steel door at the end of the hallway, the Father saw three rusted pick-up trucks and a couple of four-wheelers parked out back. Apart from those, his own sedan, and some empty beer cans, there was nothing else. Reverend Blake was gone. Perhaps he had a change of heart. Shannon, shaking his head as he made his way to the car, felt hefty arms grasp around his head and neck from behind. Stars flashed behind his fluttering eyes.

Before Shannon passed out, he heard Reverend Blake rasp, "Father... forgive me, for I'm about to sin."

***

Father Shannon awoke in a wooden chair with his arms strapped behind his back. He was in a gray room with a crimson-painted floor, and seated uncomfortably close to a dinner table. The smell of stewed meat hung in the air, and a boiling pot bubbled somewhere outside the room. He was unsure how long he'd been unconscious. The window in the room had the shades pulled down, but light seeped in, letting him know it was not yet evening.

Across from him, Reverend Blake tore stringy meat off the bone with his front teeth. Barbecue sauce dribbled out of his mouth, down his chin, and dripped onto his white, button-up shirt. He waved a large, chunky remote at the screen of an old box television set. The static screen hissed at a high volume. The reverend laughed at the television.

With shallow breath, Shannon strained, "Where am I? What's going on here?"

Blake answered, "I'm eating." He guffawed again at the television. "I gotta tell you, Father... that Andy Griffith is something else, ain't he?"

"He—he sure is."

Reverend Blake gazed at the black and white bumblebee pattern on the screen with a satisfied smirk.

"Yeah, really. Andy Griffith. He sure is great."

The reverend's face dropped to a stone-like stare. He muted the TV and grit his teeth. "You think I'm crazy."

"I don't think you're crazy." Shannon feigned sincerity by furrowing his brow, though the slight uptick in his voice gave him away. He cleared his throat. "I, um, wondered. Have you seen my phone?"

The reverend checked his pocket. "Huh, I do have your phone. Must have picked it up by accident." He slid the phone on Father Shannon's side of the table.

Shannon breathed out slowly as his neck pulsed. "I really don't think you're crazy. Desperate maybe? Clinging to life? This must be so h—"

"Cut the bull, Father!" Blake's half-eaten rib clanged onto the plate. He paused with a deep breath. "I know the protocols. Agree with the aggressor, de-escalate the situation? I used to be a surgeon, you know. Dealt with the unhinged all the time." He pressed a button and the static screamed once again.

"You don't say. I considered becoming a nurse in my younger days. As clergy, I suppose I'm still saving lives. What about you?" Shannon tried to keep the conversation light as he subtly tried to loosen his bonds.

The reverend smirked as he reminisced. "I used to be a damned good surgeon, but then my hands began to shake at the operating table... whenever the hunger hit. You're insightful. That's really where my confession begins."

"I'm all ears." Shannon continued moving his wrists, trying to loosen them from his binding, but the zip tie held them together. The chair seemed heavy, he couldn't make it move, and his fear of being caught fought him.

With a hearty chuckle, Reverend Blake eyed Father Shannon. "You're so much more than that."

"I'm glad to be."

Licking his lips, Reverend Blake said, "I gave up the drink, but the shakes still hexed me. That's when I got the calling and had to give up the practice."

"Into the ministry?"

Sweat formed on Blake's forehead, and his teeth began to chatter. "No... I don't know how to exactly phrase it."

Despite the situation, Father Shannon's heart moved with compassion. "I won't pry. You don't need to share anything you're not comfortable with."

Blake tilted his head back, cracked his neck, and loosened his shoulders. "I wanna be a man of my word. Maybe if I just talk about the last time."

"The last time?" Shannon gently pulled with his wrists to see if he could slip off his binding. There was not much give, and he couldn't move his legs.

"Last week, I saw poor Mrs. Greenwich, all by herself, carrying a heavy bag of groceries. I wouldn't be a man of God if I didn't offer to help carry them. Her house is only a couple blocks past mine."

Father Shannon nodded. "That sounds like the right thing to do."

"I agree. I agree. As we passed my house, the shakes began again." Reverend Blake scratched the back of his neck like he had an itch caused by a mosquito. "It didn't take much convincing. An invite to tea in the preacher's home? But I couldn't stop my-myself."

Concerned over what was coming next, Shannon sat still, silent.

Reverend Blake walked to the corner of the room as if he were reliving the moment and acted out as he shared. "I grabbed hold of her neck and squeezed. At first, she looked alarmed, but then peace came when her carotid stopped throbbing." He carried his chair next to Father Shannon, sat down, and whispered, "But that's not good."

Father Shannon fought the urge to shudder. "I agree."

"I knew you'd understand. If the blood remains in the body, then the meat can't be eaten. I carried her upstairs to this room immediately and drained her blood before preparing her."

Shannon held his breath and inadvertently turned his head away in disbelief.

"But I suppose that will be the second to last time. Anyway, it's finally caught up with me. I have a prion disease, and I'm going to die. I'm glad you're joining me in my final meal, Father." A sizzle came from outside the room. "My pot is boiling over. Thank you... for listening. I'm so relieved to get that off my chest." He patted the father's head as he exited the room.

Shannon's heart raced. He couldn't get his wrists free, the zip ties wouldn't loosen, and the pain from the plastic cutting into his wrists was too great for him to try any longer. If he could get the chair to fall and break, he could be free enough to call the police on his phone. Still unable to move his legs, he shifted his bottom back and forth until the chair began to rock.

Staring over his shoulder at the door, he continued.

Each shift tilted him a little more... and a little more.

Until the chair tipped back... but then stopped.

"Whoa, whoa. You'll hurt yourself that way, my friend." Reverend Blake righted the chair and pulled it back. "You weren't trying to leave, were you?"

"I've heard your confession. May you find forgiveness in the Lord. I think it's time I leave."

Blake flashed a long knife next to Shannon's right eye. "All you had to do is ask." He cut the zip tie loose.

"And my legs?" Shannon added.

Blake scoffed, "Your legs aren't tied, but the anesthetic should wear off in a few hours."

Shannon looked down at his legs, bandaged above the knees with nothing below them. In silent shock, his face contorted with anguish-ridden terror.

While Father Shannon sobbed, Reverend Blake smashed the smartphone with the handle of the knife. "I guess you're staying after all." He nodded his head, agreeing with his thoughts. "You'll provide at least three days. You're a praying man. You can always pray the disease kills me first. Thanks to you, my next meal is ready... and I'm dying of hunger."

Flesh and Blood

Bryn Eliesse

Humid and hot, his breath pants into my ear, accompanied by the slick rasp of his tongue. The wet muscle grazes my earlobe before sliding between his thin lips, erasing the evidence of blood from my skin—even as the sharp tang invades my nostrils. A violent shiver runs down my spine.

"Miss me, sweet sibling," he murmurs softly in the lowest octave that he can muster. Not a question, so much as a fact.

Lifting a corner of my mouth into the semblance of a smile, I reply, "I always do." The words leave an ashen taste in my already dry mouth. A wave of nausea envelops me as his hand meets steel; still warm with my body's heat from the day's harvest.

Index finger caressing the serrated edge, he does not deign to give me a response. Though he never does. Pitch-black iris' train on my face before his teeth bare into a crude mockery of a smile.

The blade glints, catching the dim light of the cabin as he brings it closer and closer to my face. I fall still. Cold steel kisses my skin. He slowly slides the blade from my cheekbone to rest on my tightly clamped lips before descending my neck to trace my collarbone.

A bright tune fills the silent cabin as my brother hums to himself, turning his attention to the workshop table before us. With his gaze averted, air floods my lungs in a silent gasp. The sensation of the blade's edge lingers, slipping with silent strokes along my flesh. Prickles of fear race from the blade's path all the way down to my frigid fingers.

I can only watch my brother with impending horror. Using the same blade, he mirrors the path from my skin onto the corpse before us— only this time with pressure. Cheekbone... Lips... Neck... Collarbone... Dark coagulated blood spills from the ripped flesh, dribbling in fragrant globules down the side of the still warm corpse onto the observation table.

All my conscious effort goes into keeping a neutral expression as he turns to me. His cheeks stretch so wide that his fanatic joy overshadows the malicious darkness of his gaze. I am unable to look away from the dark tint of his lips and the smears of red marring his pristine teeth.

He slams the knife into the table; my toes curl in my threadbare boots, fighting a full-body flinch. With glee still shining in his obsidian eyes, he turns to me.

Grasping my cheeks with a bloodied hand, he pushes them together, reminiscent of our childhood. I feel the sticky blood smear against my skin while he holds my gaze. "I love you. Wish your big bro good luck!" The hand does not withdraw. Instead, the pressure strengthens, almost forcing my jaw open. He waits until, with a low voice, I answer, "I love you too. Good luck."

His mouth quirks into a playful smile, the bloodlust's glee still apparent on his face. He slaps me as I am released. Dragging a finger through the dense pool of cooling blood, he draws a misshapen heart on the table. Licking a finger with a merry pop, he turns for the door, practically skipping into the tundra-like terrain, shouting, "Be back soon with another!" The door slams with a note of finality.

Cotton, I think numbly; my ears feel stuffed with cotton. Blinking a few times, I attempt to alleviate the sharp flashes of light illuminating my peripheral vision. The tips of my fingers are noticeably numb as I flex my hand. In my mouth, my tongue feels too large, weighing heavily. The floor tilts below me, and I come all at once to the conclusion that I am about to pass out.

Sinking down onto the sopping dirt floor, my hand slams onto the observation table, clinging to some kind of purchase. Nostrils flaring, my breath comes in short pants as I focus on the sensation of blood drying on my skin. Fresh tears make tracks through the crusting flakes of red.

Through the watery film over my eyes, I strain my neck to watch the door, though my body refuses to rise completely. The cooling blood soaks the denim covering my knees. Soon. He will be back soon. *Get up.* Get up, get up, get up...

Clawing into a standing position, I hesitate, gazing at the corpse.

Beautiful auburn hair fanning the table catches the light, dredging questions up from the recesses of my mind that I hastily dismiss. Never attach a name or story to the corpse. No questions, no answers, no obligations for justice. On a typical Tuesday night, my brother's craving for death was born from sacrifice, as he saved me from our father. My brother proved too strong for the bourbon-soaked monster, and what might have once been a weeknight brawl transformed into a lethal encounter and rainy funeral.

I clasp the blade with a shaking grip, resuming the third harvest of the day. Another day of watching the pile of corpses in the corner grow until he recycles them with a rusted shovel.

First heart, then lungs, and so forth until each specimen finds itself in a neatly labeled box for shipment. I do not know if my brother sells these parts, puts them on a dinner plate, or ships them to their family's home. I have never dared to ask.

I vaguely register the dull thud of a truck door slamming.

Then I hear another. The knife clatters on the table.

The color drains from my face as I frantically whip my head from side to side. Gaze locking onto the frosted windowpane, I race across the room, jostling the latch until I can boost myself up from the pile of corpses to climb outside. I don't bother to shut it. Bloody boot prints in the snow will guide their hunt.

Taking off into a stumbling sprint, I hear a chorus of laughter from the open window. Time slows as I scramble through the blinding blizzard. Straining, I catch the faint roar of engines from the interstate to guide my way.

I must make it this time. I must make my brother proud.

In his own twisted way, my brother has always wanted me to escape. To save him from himself. However, I have never been able to betray him, as my weakness created this monstrous version of him. Even in this gnarled and rotted form of love, he is the only person in the world who is my own.

Only when his friends come am I allowed to escape, creating their favorite pastime–hunting. And I am the best prey of all. They revel in my screams and bathe in the scent of my fear as they drag me back for their fun. I, too, am ashamedly swept away by the adrenaline of the chase. However, I can never be sure of whether I want to be caught or not.

High-pitched laughter echoes around me. The unfamiliar scent of tar and burning fuel scorches my lungs with each inhale of biting air; this is the furthest I've made it.

The swirling sounds of laughter and roaring engines makes my head spin as I slip in the snow, struggling up the steep bank to the paved road ahead. My nails crack as I find purchase on the concrete, dragging my body forward. I press a hand onto a solid barrier, lunging over... leaving a lone dark handprint behind.

As cars swerve around me, I feel air shifting. I slide to a halt in the middle of the interstate. My eyes lock on my brother and his friend; they are no longer laughing. Their eyes peer from the trees like ravenous wolves stalking their prey.

I feel poised. For what, I do not know. I assume the sirens in the distance will reach me before a car can kill me. Spreading my arms victoriously and bathing in red and blue lights, I grin triumphantly at my brother amidst the chorus of shouting officers.

Backing into the shadows, my brother and his friend retreat, fading into the darkening timber, as my torso becomes a canvas for bright strobes of light. I am forced to my knees, as manacles bite my wrists. In time, my brother will intimately know the sensation of steel on his skin. Until then, I pray his victims meet a quick and painless death. But I know my prayers will not be answered.

Take the Plunge

Séimí Mac Aindreasa

Two consecutive tours have taught me what love is.

The rickety, rust-pocked carriage jolts and we begin our ascent, your nervous squeal causing an outburst of laughter from the waiting queue.

Below us, the funfair shows off its lights as we soar: well-walked pathways, bathed in bare-bulbed glare, enticing rubes to lose their money quickly; the trailing neon lights of the different rides daring young bucks to take their chances. In the distance, we see the edges of the park trailing into darkness: the caravans and mobile homes of the hustlers and stand-owners, who make their living from our gullibility, our desire for cheap thrills.

The lights, the carny-barking competing with the calliope cacophony; the shouts and yells of different grifters on the strip, all promising the glory of cheap baubles, if only you can beat their system.

I have waited. For this time, this place. I have waited because I have a very important question for you.

You. Look at you: beauty personified; with eyes of deepest green and a smile that would cause gods to weep in envy. You, who stood by me when Pa died; who comforted me when I got my call-up papers. You, who gave me a lock of hair, just before I shipped out to Da Nang. Always you.

The smell of hotdogs and warm, buttered popcorn drifts from below as we continue our slow journey, and I am lost in your gaze. I almost blurt out my proposition, there and then. But not yet! Not yet. Not until we're at the top.

Rising higher, I remember you in school: your beautiful ringlets; the chequered hairband you always wore. The cute dimples you had - still have.

We near the peak. We can see across the whole county from here, little towns marked out by a myriad of tiny lights in the gathering dusk.

Khe Sanh suddenly flashes across my eyes: the lights below briefly becoming phosphorous rounds, snaking towards their targets. My finger tightens against an imagined M60 trigger-

The carriage sways, hanging on oiled supports, bringing me back to the present. We reach the pinnacle of the ride.

I turn to you nervously. Your look of surprise is almost believable as I drop to one knee before you. You know. You were expecting this.

What you aren't expecting, is me pulling a knife from my boot.

"I know," I whisper, as the blade sends multi-coloured reflections dancing across your startled face. "I know about you and Roger. And Billy, and all the others. I – know."

Your face – your beautiful face – cracks as the realisation floods in and shock blanches it to marble white.

Two consecutive tours *have* taught me what love is. *Love is a battlefield.*

"Here's my proposal. Either you jump, right now, or I carve you up, like I carved up those fucking animals in My Lai. Decide."

Your pathetic whimper is cut short as I stand, lurching the carriage violently.

"So," I roar. "What's it gonna be?"

You decide, and my heart soars as yours plummets.

The Monster Within

Mikayla Hill

No one told me that there would be a rush, an unbelievable high. They warn you of the hunger, the lack of control, and the loss of normalcy. I never expected to see smells or be able to diagnose a patient through the sound of their pulse, the fluttering beat of the blood through their veins. For the first time since my diagnosis, I found myself filled with hope, instead of sorrow. Tomorrow would be the true test, the final day of the fifteen-day quarantine.

The old tales spoke of moons, but this was no lunar condition. Recent medical studies showed that each case was different, and while some did have a monthly occurrence, others would be affected nightly, or only under times of duress. The old tales got a lot of things wrong, from Alicorns to Zombies, the lore was muddled by time and disbelief.

The asylum's artificial dawn woke me as the speakers piped in the tinny sounds of recorded songbirds. My head snapped around as I heard the soft footsteps making their way up the hall. The metallic click of the door unlocking brought me to my feet, and the smell of meat drew me out of the room, and I joined the shuffling queue headed to the dining space.

The human guard reeked of silver, though the sluggish sound of his heart was more of a deterrent than any weaponry. I stopped short, the person behind me muttered curses as they crashed into my motionless body, *had I truly thought of the guard as "human"? Had I seriously thought of him as food?* I forced myself to move forward and re-join the line of hungry monsters.

The hope that had filled me last night was gone, and the leaden feeling of dread took its place. With a filled plate, I took my seat among the other patients.

"Your last day, innit, doc?" A beady-eyed fellow asked, his head tilted quizzically, his eyes shining with intensity. I felt my hackles bristling under his stare, but I nodded anyway, my mouth too full of beef to speak. He continued, undeterred by my lack of reply, "What are you in for anyway? I don't believe you told us. A Warlock cursed me. Time after time, I tried telling them it's not a proper condition, but would they listen? I've just got two more days, then I'm outta here."

I hastily swallowed, shaking my head. "I was performing surgery, nicked myself on a rib. Didn't expect to test positive." I sighed, shrugged my shoulder and ran my hand through my hair. "Must've fainted or something, because the next thing I remember was waking up in here." I leant in close and continued in a whisper, "I don't remember if they even told me what I caught." I gave a wry chuckle. "Guess I'll find out soon enough."

The day seemed to crawl by, the sound of human heartbeats grew louder, and I found myself wondering what human flesh would taste like. It was only mid-afternoon when I retreated to my room, the empty cell filled with beautiful silence. I sat cross-legged on the bed, a meditative position I hadn't had to use in years. I closed my eyes and focused on relaxing my body, one muscle at a time until I felt the tension melt away. *I don't want to eat people. I don't want to eat people. I don't want to eat people.* I repeated this phrase, this wish, almost like a mantra. *I don't want to be a monster; I am a doctor. I should be helping people, not wanting to devour them.*

I don't know how much time passed before I heard the sound of someone approaching my cell. I could smell them, they smelled of sugar and sunshine. The door swung inward, and I opened my eyes. There stood an unfamiliar nurse, clipboard and tray in hand. "Time for your final evaluation, Doctor Spalling."

I stood and the nurse calmly indicated that I should remove my shirt. Frowning, I complied but not without question. "Is there a point to undressing?"

She merely waved her hand at the tray, where a stethoscope, syringe, and other basic medical equipment sat. "Simple examination, Doctor, and a final blood test."

I couldn't help but grimace. The taking of blood always made me feel queasy. A laughable trait as a doctor, but it was not uncommon.

The nurse peered into my ear with the otoscope, her warm breath gently stirred the hair at the nape of my neck. "Do you want to forget about being a monster?" The whispered question surprised me, I nodded in reply. "I can make it like you were never even here, I can make you as normal as you felt when you first awoke here."

I could feel the buoyant sensation of hope creeping back. "How?" It was a shaky, breathy word. Filled with hope, loss, and disbelief.

A smile burst from her face, the smell of sunshine filled my nostrils, and an energy crackled through the room. "Majik!"

That single word boomed forth, no louder than a whisper, yet deafening as the power in it thrummed through my body. "Majik comes with a sacrifice, a price, always. What do you ask?"

The nurse chuckled, "Suspicious, are we? It isn't much, simply surrender your memories of this experience. You would never remember your time as a monster, nor this place at all."

I scoffed at that; it seemed too good to be true. I didn't want to remember picturing eating people, or the smell of fear. I would miss the heightened senses, but the trade-off was more than worth it to be normal again. I gave a decisive nod. "Deal."

The nurse seized my head in her hands, her fingers digging slightly into the skin around my temple. "Hoc tempore redire. Da mi memoriam ejus. Iterum." With the last word echoing through my head, the world faded to black.

I felt consciousness return gradually. Whispers filtered down to my ears and the light slowly filled the space behind my eyelids. I forced my eyes to open, the unfamiliar roof coming into focus. Blinking, I sat up gingerly, testing for injury. I seemed fine. My attention went outward and I saw two people looking towards me, mid-conversation. The silver-haired man saw that I was awake and put his hand up to stop the younger man from talking further, then stepped closer.

"Doctor Spalling, how are we feeling? I am afraid there has been an incident. You seem to have contracted something during your last surgical procedure. You will be safe here during the standard fifteen-day transitional period. Welcome to Infiniti Asylum."

Tricks, No Treats

Kerr Pelto

"Alexa, play 'Vampires Will Never Hurt You' by My Chemical Romance."

Jerry gyrated his hips to the music reverberating throughout the cathedral-ceilinged great room. Candlelight threw ghostly dancing shadows on the walls. He hoped his attention to detail, creating a sensual ambiance, would be appreciated. He couldn't think of a better treat on All Hallows Eve than spending the evening with the delicious Candy.

He walked into the hallway and paused in front of a mirror to adjust his pointy teeth. A scream caught in his throat when an identical vampire materialized behind him. Jerry whirled around, making the sign of the cross in an effort to ward off evil.

"What are *you* doing here?!"

"Did you not think I'd find you, Jere?"

"Karl, now's not a good time. I'm expecting my date in about ten minutes." With his back pressed against the wall, Jerry inched his way into the kitchen.

Karl followed, a deranged look in his eyes. "So, the time *was* right for you to kill my wife? You thought you were smarter than her, that she wouldn't find the discrepancies in the General Ledger and realize you'd been embezzling from our company? You thought you'd get away with it, didn't you?"

Sweat crept down Jerry's forehead, streaking his meticulous vampiric makeup. He leaned back against the countertop, hands behind him, and clutched the cold marble for stability.

"She would have destroyed you." Karl stepped in closer, shortening the gap between them. "Now I'm going to do that for her." Light danced off the razor-sharp knife raised above Karl's head before it was plunged into Jerry's heart, ending a horrified scream.

A warm feeling of satisfaction flooded Karl's body and satiated his desire for revenge. He cleaned off the large knife and returned it to the knife block. The loud door chime startled him.

"Trick or Treat!" yelled the excited children standing outside the door.

Karl exited the kitchen, threw open the front door, pelted candy at the three little ghosts, and bared his teeth. The terrified children screamed and fled, tripping over tombstones littering the yard. Karl exhaled his irritation, then looked down at Jerry's attempt at a makeshift coffin. Grabbing the skeleton nestled inside, he crammed it into a large trash bin beside the garage.

Perspiration soaked his white, ruffled shirt as he struggled to drag Jerry's body out the front door. He groaned, hoisting the lifeless body into the coffin. Picking up a nearby flowerpot of chrysanthemums, he smashed the contents on Jerry's face so it wouldn't be recognized.

Headlights rounded the corner as a red BMW Coupe pulled into the driveway. Bloodred stilettos emerged from the driver's side, followed by a svelte, auburn-haired vampiress. Candy swung her hips erotically and sauntered up the steps, stopping next to the casket.

Karl relinquished the thoughts of what he'd just done and, instead, fixated on the luscious body before him. The tight-fitting costume and plunging neckline left nothing to the imagination.

Candy looked up from the body in the casket, licked her full, ruby lips, and spoke in a silky voice, "Nice touch, Jerry. The blood looks real."

Karl shrugged. "The knife helped."

"Why does your voice sound different?"

"Laryngitis?"

Candy brushed against him as she entered the house. Karl turned out the porch lights to discourage further interruptions, then followed her into the kitchen where Jerry's ghoulish delectables were spread out on the black marble countertop. Karl's evening was taking an unexpected yet desirable twist. Candy could turn out to be a real treat. He came in close and hovered behind her.

She felt Karl's hot breath on the back of her neck and recoiled at his unspoken intentions. "I know what you did."

Karl was confused. Did she realize the body in the coffin was real? Did she know he wasn't Jerry?

"Sorry, I don't know what you mean. What do you think I've done?"

"Don't act innocent, Jerry. The tall brunette with the violet eyes spilled the beans at my party last night. Said she'd had quite the fling with a Mr. Caldwell. Do you know any other Caldwells other than yourself, Jerry?"

Candy grabbed a large knife from the knife block and whirled around. She bared her fangs and shoved the sharp blade into his heart. "No one cheats on me, Jerry."

As Jerry's twin brother gurgled blood and collapsed to the floor, all he could think about was the violet-eyed bombshell he'd met the night before.

Her jealousy revenged, Candy knew where she'd hide the body. She'd just exchange it for the fake one in the casket.

All the Santas We Cannot See

Christopher Bloodworth

"Gerald, would you please grab two eggs and a box of butter from the fridge?"

Gerald was six.

"Yes ma'am."

Gerald, who was—despite his best efforts to live up to the maturity implied by his name—still only half the height needed to reach these perishables, dragged over a kitchen barstool and clambered up to retrieve the eggs and butter for his mother. He paused just before closing the refrigerator, his eyes having landed on the milk.

"Here you go, Mum. Um, can you pour me a glass of milk, please?"

"Sure, sweetie," she said, and, having transferred the items to a space on the counter where she was shortly to prepare the cookie dough, she pulled out the milk and poured Gerald a glass. He set it aside.

From his barstool vantage point, Gerald watched and encouraged his mother as she expertly whisked together all of the ingredients for the cookies that were a Christmas Eve tradition in their household. One might have assumed these cookies were intended for Santa, but Gerald, on the advice of his parents, didn't believe in such things.

The cookies were purely ritualistic—a holdover of his mother's own childhood traditions—for Gerald's was a modern family, and his parents did not hold with telling lies to their children, whatever the reason. And so, on Christmas Eve, they made cookies and left none for Santa.

Of course, Gerald had complete faith in his parents, and they had never yet given him reason to doubt their wisdom. His confidence was without question—absolute. Although, he did find there were times when, despite his certainty... it was difficult to say. Children are nothing if not outspoken about their opinions on things, and Gerald was finding that at school, his seemed far and away the minority opinion. Not that he could be so easily seduced by something as banal as peer pressure. It was just that the only other child willing to dismiss the legend of Santa so readily was a new kid—a little atheist boy named Samir, and Gerald wasn't certain he wanted him as his only ally.

When he first experienced these doubts—no, not doubts. More like follow-up questions—Gerald had decided to seek clarity on the matter from his father, who seemed to live in the family's reading chair and was, therefore, an authority on most subjects that could be found in a book.

"Dad?" he had asked tentatively, thinking how to frame the question as nonspecifically as possible. "How do you know if something is real?"

"Mmm? If something is real?" Even though he was sitting in his armchair, his father still had to look down at Gerald over the top rims of his reading glasses. "That's a pretty big question."

His father had looked up thoughtfully at the corner of the ceiling, a practice Gerald had learned not to interrupt.

"Well, I suppose the easiest way is to look at it—to get your hands on it, or even taste it if you have to. In fact, they used to test whether gold coins were real by biting on them to make sure they weren't actually gold-plated lead, which although heavy like gold, is so soft that your teeth would leave a dent in it."

Gerald wasn't sure biting Santa was an option.

"Ok. But what if you can't see it?"

His father had looked at Gerald as though thinking very hard.

"That one is a bit tougher. There *are* things we know are real even though we can't see them. We can't see air, for instance."

"But we *can feel* air, right? Isn't that like seeing it?"

His father laughed.

"Very true! Well, how about this? There's something in space called a black hole. It's a collapsed star where the gravity is so strong, light can't bounce off of it or shine from it, which means it's invisible. They're totally black, just like the space around it, so we have no way to see them or feel them, and they're so far away that you could travel for hundreds of millions of years and never reach one."

"Then how do we know they exist?" Gerald had asked skeptically.

"Precisely the question! The answer is that we know they're real because of the effect they have on the things around them! We cannot see them directly, but their gravity is so strong, it influences the stars and gasses close to them, and we *can* see those. It's like knowing it's a windy day without going outside because you see the trees swaying through the window. So even when we can't see something, we can know it's real because it has an impact on the things around it."

Gerald had thought for a moment before simply saying, "Ok. Thanks, Dad."

It wasn't that his father's answer wasn't helpful; Gerald had thought the answer quite good. So good, in fact, that he was tempted to drop the matter entirely simply because a man who knew all that about black holes in outer space millions of light-years away would certainly not be mistaken about the existence of Santa Claus. However, there was still the matter of his classmates' overwhelming opposition, as well as his skepticism of his ally, who was new and who was an atheist, and whose name was Samir. And so, with the balance of these things in mind, Gerald had decided to settle the thing in the manner suggested by his father: he would stay up and see for himself.

In the time it took for his parents to go to bed on Christmas Eve, Gerald felt like he might have completed several round trips to one of these "black holes." But, at long last, they retreated to their bedroom, and Gerald emerged from his.

He wasn't really sure how to summon Santa, if that's what one did, but he tried to go about the thing properly—if Santa didn't appear, he wanted to be absolutely sure that it wasn't because of some technicality of failed preparation. Thus, he had stolen his father's largest and thickest wool socks, and with thumbtacks, pinned them on the mantle to serve as Christmas stockings. Using the platter of leftover cookies and a TV tray, Gerald set about making a handsome display conveniently close to the fireplace, and he even arranged the cookies so that the edge of each one overlapped elegantly with the next. With a finishing touch, he added the milk, which was a simple matter of retrieving the glass his mother had poured for him earlier that evening.

Gerald wondered how long he'd been waiting. He hadn't thought to check the clock at the outset of his vigil, but it was well past midnight when he began wondering at what time he should declare the experiment a success and Santa a fraud. The seconds ticked away, and the sounds of the house seemed to be amplified in his ears. More than once he thought he heard something from inside the chimney, but nothing happened. The last time, he even went to look up into it but found the flue closed. He didn't remember any rules about flues being left open or shut, but as with the hanging of the stockings, he decided to open it, just to be safe. It creaked loudly, much louder than he'd expected, and cold air poured down from the opening and flooded the room.

Gerald's eyes watered against the frigid draft as he peeked up the chimney. Blinking away tears, he thought he could see something. In fact, he was sure of it. It was difficult to see properly, but he was certain this wasn't Santa. He didn't know how Santa would fit down the chimney—probably some magic suited to the task—but Gerald was quite sure that Santa would take up the entire cavity if and when he finally descended. Whatever this not-Santa was, it appeared to be stirring, as if Gerald's gaze had awakened it. Then, much to Gerald's alarm, something like legs slowly unfolded from the thing's body, and it began to crawl down the fireplace.

Gerald backed away from the opening, conscious not to turn his back on the creature whose legs were now blooming from the fireplace the way a rose opens its petals in a time-lapse, but black—blacker than any black Gerald had ever seen. He knew without a shadow of a doubt that *this* was a black hole, and no amount of light could ever escape it.

"You... Um, you're *not* Santa... are you?" Gerald asked bravely, with as much strength as his small voice could muster.

True, this creature was not red, round, and jolly—now that it had fully emerged and risen to its full height, it most reminded Gerald of an enormous stick bug—but on the other hand, it wasn't as if he hadn't *planned* on meeting a stranger in the chimney that evening, and it seemed rather a strong coincidence that something *else* should be making use of the chimney on Christmas Eve.

"... In a way."

It spoke slowly, its voice like a whisper, and Gerald couldn't decide if his surprise would have been greater had the creature *not* spoken. It didn't look like anything he'd seen speak before, yet the fact that it could seemed somehow... natural.

"If you don't mind my saying, you don't really *look* like Santa."

"I am not."

"Oh," Gerald said in surprise, "but you said—"

"I exist because of your Santa, but I am not him. *He* is not him. He is not anything."

"Oh, I see." Gerald said, although he didn't. "Then..." Gerald trailed off, unsure of what to say next, and to fill the silence, he opted for common politeness. "Uh, I've saved some milk and cookies for... well... I don't know if you eat these, but... you can have some... if you like." And Gerald held out the tray.

"Yesssss," it hissed, "I *am* hungry."

It was over quickly, which was nice for Gerald, who would have been sad about his fate. Sad, and not a little confused as well. For as smart as Gerald was, his schooling as a six year old was yet deficient on the subject of evolution, the principle by which this creature's species had adapted through the centuries to lay dormant in chimneys, hibernating undetected throughout the year, waiting for the one night when the myth of St. Nicholas would prompt children to sneak from their beds and lay in wait by their chimneys.

He might have reflected, had he lived, that his father's proclamation on the nature of what is true was not quite complete. For though we may pinpoint a black hole by its pull on its surroundings, until we can see or feel it, it will always be unknown to us. Except to those it swallows up—and perhaps even then—its true nature will remain a mystery, certain only to be different than we have imagined.

Vortak: Evil Wizard

James Hancock

Vortak was an evil wizard. He had a tower at the edge of the black forest in Mortissia, twenty minions to guard it, fifteen magic items in his treasury at the top and a princess from Elandar locked in the dungeons below. He was on the verge of defeating Duke Laminar of Brightmoor when a party of hired adventurers broke into his tower and set upon his minions. The princess was rescued, there were deaths on both sides, and Vortak was forced to quickly open and flee through a magic portal. The spell didn't go as planned. A fumbled casting when he really didn't need one, and Vortak was transported to an unknown world and without the means to open a new portal. Trapped! But he had survived. Now he lives in a one bedroom flat in Brighton, England, and earns his keep in the only way he can... Vortak the Incredible: Wizard For Hire. Degrading himself at music festivals and children's parties in the Sussex area.

He had been in his new life for three months; a life of gas and electricity bills, buying bread and milk from the local shop, and making small talk with his eccentric neighbour, Graham.

***

Graham knocked on Vortak's door, beamed a big smile, and held it fixed, ready for when Vortak answered. He waited. A minute passed and his jaw began to ache. He dropped the smile and reached up to knock again as the door opened. Graham's smile quickly returned as Vortak stepped into the doorway, lifting a lantern to illuminate the area and display his cold and sinister face; he stared with deep blue eyes under a heavy frown, pale skin, jet black hair and robes to match. Graham felt underdressed and inferior, with his red tracksuit, fake tanned skin, brilliantly white teeth and skinny physique.

Vortak considered how easily he could crush Graham.

Graham held up a plate of freshly cooked homemade brownies. "I thought you might like some homemade brownies. Fresh out the oven." Graham continued to beam his exaggerated smile.

Vortak looked at them and then back at Graham, thinking for a moment. "I accept," Vortak said, taking the brownies with his free hand and slamming the door shut with his foot. Graham waited for two minutes, but Vortak didn't return.

Vortak walked into his living room, which had all the modern furnishings yet was lit by several lanterns and dozens of candles. He placed the lantern on a small table, and sat in a comfortable chair with brownies on lap. He picked up the first one, was about to take a bite, and a vibrating buzz sounded from under him. He jumped, startled, and dropped the plate on the floor.

"Son of a witch!" he yelled and instinctively unleashed flames from his hands at the scattered brownies. He quickly calmed himself as the buzz sounded again, and reached under his robes to pull a mobile phone from his trousers pocket.

Vortak placed the phone to his ear whilst stamping out the small carpet fire near his feet. "Who calls me at this hour?" Vortak spoke with an intimidating tone.

He listened. "Yes. Next Saturday at one o'clock. Let me check my diary." Vortak paused, leaned forward and picked up a non-charred brownie. "I am available. What age will your daughter be, and how many infants should I expect?"

Vortak took a bite of the brownie, nodding as he listened to the information.

"Send an electronic message to this device after the conversation has ended, and specify your address. I shall be there on time. I accept cash and cash only!" He ended the call.

Vortak got up and walked across his living room, taking another bite of the brownie and making a noise of appreciation as he entered his kitchen. He lifted a Brighton Pier fridge magnet and pulled a sheet of paper free from his fridge door; a thermometer style goal chart, with four thousand as the objective and just under one hundred coloured in. A long way to go. Vortak mused over the words at the top of the page – *Minions required to conquer the lands of East Sussex.*

Vortak shook his head, disappointed. "Eight-year-olds. Damn them and their weak bodies! Oh how I despise children and their..." His phone buzzed and vibrated again, causing him to drop the sheet of paper and last of his brownie.

"Damn this cursed communication device!" he yelled as he pulled the phone from his pocket and checked a text message. His rage calmed.

"Oh good, that's just around the corner."

***

An eighth birthday party for Maisie. "Hire a wizard," Muriel's friend had advised, and that's what she did. Hopefully it would be a party her daughter would remember. Ten children sat on the living room floor, staring up at the black robed individual before them.

"Who knows what a Necromancer is?" asked Vortak. Three hands went up.

"Ugly child at the front." Vortak pointed at a spotty child. Half of the children were shocked by Vortak's comment, and the other half sniggered, covering their mouths to stop themselves from laughing out loud. The spotty child was understandably embarrassed.

"Someone who can summon skeletons," the spotty child said, worried he might get ridiculed again.

Muriel had been making sandwiches in the kitchen, and unsure of what she had just heard, moved to the living room doorway to keep an eye on things.

"Sort of," said Vortak. "It is someone who can animate the dead. Zombies, ghouls, even wraiths if the Necromancer is powerful enough. Now, does anyone have a dead pet with them?"

Muriel frowned and crossed her arms, edging into the room a little to let Vortak see she was there watching him. Seeing where this was going. None of the children raised a hand, and all looked understandably confused.

"Never mind," said Vortak, thinking for a moment. "Any live pets? I can still make it work."

Maisie's hand went up. "Spoiled girl." Vortak pointed at Maisie.

"My cat died. Jemima. She is buried at the bottom of the garden." Maisie was unsure of herself.

"Excellent!" said Vortak, waving a hand through the air. "Shovel." And a shovel appeared in his hand. The children gawped and gasped in amazement. Vortak passed the shovel to Maisie, who gave a grin of importance and put it on the carpet beside her. It was too big to keep hold of.

Vortak rubbed his chin, thinking. "The ground is a bit hard this time of year. Pickaxe," he said, and a pickaxe appeared in his hand. The children all clapped.

"You'll need to choose a friend to help you." Vortak passed the pickaxe to Maisie, who placed it with the shovel. She looked back to see all nine of her friends looking at her with their hands up, desperately trying to get her attention. Pick me!

"No. Sorry... can we move away from this please?" Muriel interjected.

Vortak nodded. "Maybe you'd like to help me. I need an assistant for my next trick."

As Muriel made her way around the gathering of infants, Vortak rummaged in his holdall bag of props and produced a fist-sized rock; rough and uncut gemstone that glistened with shades of gold and purple. Muriel stepped up beside Vortak as he pulled a coffee table closer to him and placed the gemstone on top. All ten children gazed at the stone in wonder.

Muriel leaned in close to whisper so only Vortak could hear her. "This is a child's party. If you want to get paid..." Vortak cut her sentence short...

"Paralyse," Vortak said, and waved his hand in front of Muriel's face. She collapsed to the floor, stiff as a board and unable to move. Vortak turned his attention back to his mesmerised audience.

"This is the shard of suggestion," Vortak said. "You will hear my words and remember them, for they are important to you." The children continued to stare at the shard of suggestion. Muriel continued to lie paralysed on the carpet by Vortak's feet.

Vortak returned to his holdall bag as he spoke, rummaging through it, looking for something, "You will take these purple sashes and... Oh crap! I've forgotten the bloody sashes." Vortak stopped looking and thought for a moment.

"The next time you get the opportunity to do some craft activities with friends or your parents, you will make a purple sash. Then you shall put it in a safe place and await the trigger words." The children remained under Vortak's spell, staring at the shard of suggestion. "You will hear them on the radio, or on the television. Or someone might read them in the newspaper. And you will hear my name, 'Vortak'. And you will hear of magic and death. When you hear these three words together, you will don your purple sashes, arm yourselves and rise up. You will come to me. Seek me out, joining with other purple sashes you meet, and kill anyone who gets in your way. Minions of Vortak, do you understand?"

"Yes, Vortak. We understand," the children spoke in unison and without emotion.

"Now repeat the trigger words back to me," Vortak commanded.

"Vortak! Magic! Death!" The children spoke the words loud and clear.

"Good," said Vortak in an upbeat manner, and picked up the shard of suggestion. "Now then. None of you will remember this spell. Including you, Mum. You will all think I was an excellent wizard and tell your friends they want to hire me. And you're back!" Vortak clicked his fingers and everyone became themselves once again. Including Muriel.

"Took a bit of a tumble there, Mrs Barker." Vortak helped Muriel to her feet. "That will be one hundred pounds please." Vortak held out his hand. The children burst into applause and whooped cheers of appreciation.

Muriel smiled. "Let me get my handbag."

***

Six years later.

Vortak stood in the lantern light of his kitchen, leaning over the worktop and colouring in the top of his thermometer chart. Four thousand minions, ready and waiting to be activated.

"It is time! Time to venture forth and make myself known. Time to strike!" Vortak bellowed a sinister laugh... "Muahahahahaha!" There was a knock at his door.

Graham waited, with lamb hotpot in hand and a smile on his face, as Vortak opened his door. "Lamb hotpot," Graham said cheerfully.

"Really Graham? It's been six years. You don't need to keep doing this." Vortak studied the Pyrex dish and inhaled the aroma. It looked and smelt good.

"Just making sure you get a hot meal once in a while. And not one from a microwave," Graham said. "You look happy today, Vortak. Something good to report?"

Vortak smiled. "Yes. This afternoon I achieved an important goal. A task which has taken six years to complete." He thought for a second and then nodded a confirmation of his decision. "In fact, I can think of nobody better to be my first."

"Ooh," said Graham, excited. His dazzling white smile widened.

Vortak waved his hand in front of Graham's face. "It is time for you to get your purple sash, Graham. Vortak! Magic! Death!"

Graham's smile dropped, but he didn't move. Both men stared at each other. Vortak frowned, unsure how Graham was unaffected by the spell.

"It's true. You are the one," Graham whispered.

Realising the potential threat facing him, Vortak quickly waved a hand before Graham and began uttering magic incantations, but was stopped as Graham threw the contents of the Pyrex dish into Vortak's face. Vortak screamed!

Graham dropped the dish as Vortak wiped lamb hotpot from his eyes.

"Aargh! It burns!" Vortak cried.

The door to number twenty, opposite, opened and old Mrs Crabtree appeared in the doorway. The nosy neighbour listened to many a corridor conversation behind her closed door, but this one needed to be seen.

"The Shadow! Archmage Hemlock said you would come." Graham quickly moved aside as Vortak cast a spell.

"Disintegrate!" Vortak bellowed, and waved his hand at Graham. Due to his blurred vision, Vortak missed his target. A pile of ash fell onto the welcome mat where Mrs Crabtree had been standing.

Graham lunged forward and slammed the palm of his hand against Vortak's chest. "Death!" Graham yelled, and Vortak fell. Lifeless. Killed by a powerful counter-spell. The wizards' duel was over in a matter of seconds.

Graham pulled out his mobile phone and quickly made a call. "Put me through to the Sussex Wizards and Warlocks Guild. Archmage Hemlock." Graham picked up his Pyrex dish as he listened. He rubbed his fingerprints from it and threw it down beside Vortak's body. "Then give him a vital message. Extremely important. Tell him Master Mage Graham Goldcrest has confirmed his suspicions, and The Shadow is no more."

Graham ended the call, closed Vortak's and Mrs Crabtree's doors, and headed back to his flat.

***

Graham cracked an egg and added it to the bowl of flour, sugar and raisins. He picked up a spoon and started mixing the contents. His attention was drawn away from his recipe as he heard an interesting 'coming up' story from his television in the next room. He left the kitchen, stirring the bowl of ingredients as he walked into his living room. Graham always had the news on, and Robert and Jill were sat side by side as always, keeping him up to date with recent events. Young, attractive, fashionable... a great double act who timed their alternate lines to perfection.

Robert's piece had caught Graham's ear. "And in local news, the people of Sussex were shocked at the sudden *Death* of much-loved wizard, *Vortak* the Incredible, who died on Thursday. He suffered a heart attack whilst at his flat in Brighton. His *Magic* will be greatly missed." Robert paused and looked at Jill. It was her turn, yet she stared ahead blankly.

Somewhat thrown by the unexpected mistake, Robert continued where Jill should have taken over, "The funeral will be held tomorrow at Saint Bartholomew's..." Robert was distracted by Jill, who had put her handbag on the news desk and was removing a long piece of purple cloth from within.

Robert gave an uncomfortable laugh and looked off camera for help.

Standing up, Jill placed the purple sash over her shoulder and reached into her handbag again.

"Is everything okay, Jill?" Robert asked, and looked back at the camera with a smile intended to reassure the viewers. Without emotion, Jill pulled a can of mace spray from her handbag, turned to Robert, and sprayed him in the eyes. Robert screamed!

As Robert coughed, cried out in pain, and tried to rub his eyes clean, Jill produced an extendable police baton from her handbag, swiped down to fully extend it, and hit Robert across the back of the head with a great deal of force. Robert slumped over the news desk... unconscious.

Graham's jaw dropped in shock as he watched Jill casually walk off screen and the television channel blip to darkness as it went off air.

Stunned, Graham's attention remained fixed upon the blank TV screen. Moments later, he snapped out of it; a screeching car from a nearby street pulled him back into the here and now. A distinct smashing sound followed the screech.

There was a scream from somewhere in the building, followed by a car alarm and what sounded like a gunshot from outside. Graham hurried over to his window and looked down at the streets below. A dozen youths wearing purple sashes were smashing a police car with bricks and bats. In the distance, a tall building's windows shattered and flames licked through. A flash of light was followed by an explosion echoing from miles away, and the droning whir of a police helicopter as it flew overhead. Horrified, Graham stared from his window. Stared at the escalating chaos. The beginnings of Vortak's uprising was underway and moving fast.

"Son of a witch," Graham whispered.

The Architect

Jonathan Braunstein

The air was filled with the sweet aroma of tobacco as Christian puffed his pipe and reviewed applicants. He unceremoniously dumped the ashes in the ashtray and eased up from his wooden chair. "Gentlemen, we have room for one more student, but only a few remaining applicants."

Jonas whispered to Leon, "Scraping the bottom of the barrel, huh?"

Leon's rotund face jiggled as he yawned. "We've been here for hours. Does it matter who we choose?"

"Perhaps?" Jonas adjusted his thin-rimmed glasses and glanced at the list.

Christian continued, "This next applicant is—"

Jonas rose to his feet. "No, not him again!"

"You have something you'd like to say?"

"I don't understand why we're considering him a second time. The boy applied last year, and we told him no. I doubt he's improved."

Christian looked down at the application papers. "He's passed the initial exams, despite not finishing his secondary education. His benefactor, Samuel Morgenstern, has personally written to us. Take a look. Here's a handwritten note requesting our consideration."

Jonas scanned the missive. "Christian, are we now allowing local business owners to affect our illustrious institution?"

"If they are willing to support the arts? Yes, we are."

"Very well. Let's see if this merits our time."

Christian passed around drawings. "Here is a series of sketches from his portfolio. He calls these *My Father's Land*."

Leon held up a sample in the fading sunlight. "Hmm. His composition is decent. He has a good sense of positive and negative space."

Christian walked around the room and lit each oil lamp so everyone could see better before the darkness of evening set in.

Jonas tossed a drawing across the table. "Where are the people?"

"There are a few in the illustration I'm holding," Leon answered.

Jonas snatched it and squinted. "I guess. Don't they seem..."

"Like an afterthought?"

"Yes! An afterthought. If we compared this to lively work, like a drawing from Käthe Kollwitz, we would throw these out. We can't enroll him."

"Are we seeking masters or are we enrolling students?" Christian asked.

"Yes, we seek students, but don't we want influencers? Leaders who can create movements, like Matisse or Picasso!"

Christian raised an eyebrow and fluttered his hand toward the back of the room. "Perhaps one of his paintings will persuade us."

Leon retrieved a stretched canvas from the stack of paintings in the corner and placed it on a large wooden easel.

The men gathered around the monochromatic study of a stately building painted in various browns.

"Any thoughts?" Christian asked.

Jonas nodded vehemently. "Now I am fully convinced."

Leon coughed. "You are?"

"Yes. I am convinced... that he's not a true artist."

"The painting has some merit," Christian noted.

"Is it painted well? Yes, it is..."

"But?"

"His use of shading is fine. Line, form, and proportion are extraordinary. I believe if we were standing at the Hofbräuhaus, this painting would be grander than the actual building. Once again, however, there are no people, no expression... no vision. It feels oppressive. Yes, I've made up my mind."

Christian stepped in front and observed a little closer. "Unfortunately, Leon, I have to agree with Jonas. Perhaps he should be an architect."

They went back to their respective seats.

"Gentleman, here is my assessment. His artwork is devoid of all life. Perhaps he doesn't care about such things. This is not where he belongs. Wouldn't you agree?"

"Absolutely," Jonas said.

"And you, Leon?"

Leon picked up a drawing from the table and sighed. "Yes, I agree."

"I will draft the letter." With resignation, Christian dipped his pen in the inkwell.

"Let's not discourage the boy, but rather encourage him as to where his talents lie. I believe he could be a master architect in the future," Leon said.

He read aloud as he wrote.

October 8, 1908

Dear Mr. Hitler,

Regarding your application to the Vienna Academy of Fine Arts, we regret to inform you that we will not be admitting you. As in the past, we find your sample drawings unsatisfactory. There are too few heads. We find the human element sorely lacking. Perhaps you should abandon your pursuit of painting and instead consider a career as an architect.

Secondary education for mathematics would be required. We recommend you apply to our School of Architecture once those conditions are met.

If this is not favorable to you, I'm sure other organizations are willing to recruit you in pursuit of your dreams. Best of luck to you.

Sincerely,

Christian Griepenkerl
Admission Representative
Vienna Academy of Fine Arts

"Well put. Let's move on to the next applicant, and may that be the last we see of that Hitler fellow. Gentlemen, I recommend we visit the new beer hall in Wieden when we're done," Jonas said.

Leon gave a hearty, "Here here!"

Christian grinned and held up his index finger. "I believe, once again, we are all in agreement."

Human

Sarah Turner

The plan was the same as always: head to the shop, pick up a bottle of supplements, then down to Marret's Park to empty them into a bin. Her own bin was too risky, of course. It had been months now, but Maggie knew the waste collectors were still on the prowl, had seen their shadowy forms rummaging through bags and boxes every Wednesday when the light was dim and everyone was still in bed.

"Morning!" Maggie called.

Old women with rollered hair waved from dark porches as the sun spread over the horizon like a cracked egg. Across the street, figures stalked the pavements, their strides rhythmic, their pale faces forever in profile. They must have been bound for work, for cramped trains and dull offices, but she imagined them looping the same streets as if fixed to a track.

"Everyone's a stranger now," Mick said when the Ryes went. Their garden disappeared shortly after—peonies and hydrangeas smothered by tarmac that glinted like a black pool. Gone was Mrs Shenton, gone were the Walkers, gone was the nameless man with the tall conifers that seemed to pierce the sky. The only solace to be found was in the narrow terraces, their pebbledash facades forever gazing at those opposite.

At the parade of shops, mournful dogs sat tethered to bollards, and customers sipped tea at iron tables, their anaemic faces turned to the sun as it arced higher in the sky. So many times, Maggie came close to telling them they ought to be careful or else they'd burn, but she always caught herself. No one would burn anymore, she thought, conscious of the smell of sun cream on her own ageing skin like coconuts and sand and places she would never go.

Sooty headlines traipsed across the day's papers: there was a new chancellor with crow-black hair, an attempt to bridge tensions with Europe, the latest reality show winner crowned in cheap plastic. Life was getting back to normal, or so they said. She picked up a copy and pushed open the shop door.

The little bell on the frame rang out, the clapper rattling wildly. It surprised her that she missed the sound of bells. She'd never been religious—apart from once or twice a year when she sat in the dim light of Saint Matthew's—but there was a permanence to their peels that spoke of bright mornings and joints roasting. Of life before.

Mr Johnson stood before her in his customary cardigan, buttons straining at the stomach, smile thin. He had a slightly doughy appearance, as if when his days came to an end, he would be rolled out and moulded into someone new. Behind him, glass jars full of sherbet lemons and humbugs lined the wall like specimens in a lab, the once separate lozenges now melded into clusters. She pictured him at the end of the day, putting his face up to the glass as if to inspect them—eyes wide, lips thin as a knife edge.

"Good morning, Maggie!" His voice was high and clear like a whistle. "What a day to be alive!"

Who said things like that?

She nodded and began perusing the shelves, aware of his unblinking gaze following her. A loaf of white bread, a block of cheese, a chocolate bar studded with candy like shards of glass. She thought of their taste—bitter and acidic—and felt thankful for the tubs of salt stacked on her shelves back home.

Sweat formed on her upper lip, a clammy patch that she hastily wiped off. She had to focus. If Mick were there, he'd know what to do; he always took everything in his stride, always had answers she couldn't think of. But Mick was gone, and he wouldn't be coming back.

That day had been mild for spring and light had clung on far into the evening. She'd sat in her usual chair, watching darkness creep up the pebbledash of the houses opposite, draining them of all colour. Shadows rippled across their curtained windows, and she was struck by the oddness of other life, strange and independent from her own, drifting in and out of all the rooms on the street. She sat until the streetlamps went out, until the sky simmered again on the horizon and the sun rose newly minted into a dull sky. And she knew then he would never come home.

The bell rang and an old lady shuffled in, trailed by a couple of schoolchildren in sky blue jumpers. Instantly the air changed, the very atoms squashing together as if to make room for more bodies. It was best to avoid the shop when it was busy, but sometimes it couldn't be helped. The lady gave a deep nod to Mr Johnson that rippled the loose skin at her chin, and he returned it, his head bowing rigidly as if from a hinge in the neck. The woman moved slowly up the aisle, one hand raised before her, ready at any moment to snatch something from the shelves. Maggie selected a bottle of supplements she didn't need and headed to the counter.

"Have you tried the new perfume?" said Mr Johnson, his bony hand picking up a bottle full of shimmering, honey-coloured liquid.

"Ah, no, thank you."

"I insist," he said, wrapping his cold, dry fingers around her wrist, thumb pressed close to the veins that snaked like rivers. A fine mist fell onto her skin. The smell was putrid, and she had to fight against screwing up her face in disgust.

"It's lovely," she managed. "Very... floral."

He narrowed his eyes.

"Floral, you say?"

"W-well, I-yes. I'll take some thanks."

He gave an oily smile.

"Of course."

Shoes padded softly on the lino as the old lady came to stand behind her, eclipsing the daylight that poured in through the glass-panelled door. The shopping was going in the bag; all she had to do was pay, then she could get out into the air. But there was a tickling sensation in her nose—that awful perfume, no doubt. She dug her nails hard into her palm, and small red frowns appeared on her skin. Was this really it? She tried to breathe deeply, but her eyes were watering, the pressure building.

The sneeze was so loud that for a moment afterwards the shop seemed entirely quiet. The lady and children were staring at her, their faces blank. This close,

Maggie could see their skin, dry and flaking, their shallow nostrils leading nowhere.

"Lock the door, please," said Mr Johnson, although to whom Maggie wasn't sure. He was still smiling, his lips threatening to pierce his cheeks. He moved over to the telephone on the counter and jabbed at the buttons with a thin finger. As he waited for someone to answer, he kept his gaze fixed on Maggie.

"Yes. We've got a human."

Proposal

Séimí Mac Aindreasa

The creature stumbled falteringly across the room, its cracked skin oozing a yellow, malodorous ichor, a trailing leg leaving a greasy, pungent trail in the dust. The stench of grave-dirt mixed with the dust of centuries, and as it opened its mouth, wriggling maggots escaped past a bloated, blistered tongue over grey, broken teeth. The tattered remains of a filthy suit covered emaciated, mould-mottled skin; a gore-covered handkerchief, stiff with crusted effluence, dangled garishly from the torn breast pocket.

The young couple in the centre of the room ignored it, their shouting bringing ancient cobwebs tumbling from the distant rafters.

In the darkness above, a shadowy form, wrapped in leathery wings, shifted the clawed feet with which it gripped the beams.

The argument carried the familiarity of a road well-travelled, with well-used barbs and favoured insults. The girl's voice was currently the main driver on this oft-travelled route.

"At least Terry has a good job; he doesn't pretend he's a writer!"

"Neither do I!"

"Good, because you're crap at it!"

"Now come on! You know I'm just waiting for that one break!"

"And how long have you been waiting? The magician kid in your first story must be all grown up now, with kids of his own, and they've all probably got better jobs than you!"

The man ran a frustrated hand through his perfectly groomed hair and pushed his designer spectacles back towards the bridge of his nose. The girl found herself cringing at the involuntary gesture which had always annoyed her.

"It wasn't my fault that woman stole my idea!" the man blurted out angrily.

"Oh, so she took the train all the way to Torquay, broke into our house, read your story and pissed off back to Scotland? A full five years before you wrote the bloody thing? Can you even hear yourself?"

From up high in the gloomy darkness, ancient wings unfurled slowly, and yellow eyes opened in a sallow, thin face.

"I've told you over and over, I originally mentioned my idea for a story about a kid with magical powers on a chat site, way before that. She must have seen it!"

"Would this be the same chat site I found on your computer? The one you said was for writers, but seemed to consist of young twenty-something girls and creepy older guys like you? That chat site?"

"No! I mean – you got that all wrong! That site wasn't about anything like that: it was all about people who were interested in–"

"Oh, I know what they were interested in, and it certainly wasn't your stupid story, which you definitely stole from that woman!"

Above, gnarled claws tightened, digging deeper grooves into the ancient timbers.

"Let's not go over all that again, it's in the past – water under the bridge!"

"Believe me – if we were near water, I'd bloody drown you!"

"Oh yes, very good, friggin' hilarious! What about you and that guy at the party? 'Oh, you're a plumber? God, I need someone to call round and fix our sink, 'cos my husband's useless at that sort of thing.' What was all that about?"

"Can you fix the sink? Can you? No, you can't. So, what's wrong with me asking someone who can?"

"You weren't asking him round for that, and besides, your cousin's a plumber!"

Ragged claws loosened their grip on the beam; wings stretched back along a spine arched, ready for the swoop. A low, snarling hiss escaped thin lips...

"Ahem, excuse me?"

The ghoul paused in its shambling approach. Its remaining, filmy eye watched the two mortals before it. Finally, it stretched out a thin arm and raised a skeletal hand missing two digits and trailing translucent ribbons of parchment-like skin. From its graveyard mouth, a short, dusty cough emerged, dislodging a green fly, bloated from its feasting on the drool congealing on the scabrous chin. The warring couple ignored him.

"Ahem," it repeated.

The woman turned her glare on the rancid creature as if only noticing it for the first time.

"Yes?" she snapped. "Can't you see my husband and I are having a discussion?"

The thing took a startled step backwards, causing a small cloud of dust to rise up from it and another, composed of spiders and heavier detritus, to fall downwards.

"Well? She demanded. "What is it?"

The husband rolled his eyes.

"Now you're being a bitch to strangers? Friend, if I were you, I'd walk – umm, lurch – away. She's off on one."

"Off on one!? I'm not the sad creep who was making eyes at the waitress in the restaurant! I'm not the pathetic loser who always has to 'work late' with 'Debs'!"

"Not this again! Debs is just a colleague. She and I–"

With a ghastly shriek, the Harpy released its grip on the ancient beam and dropped to the floor below, slamming into the ground in a cloud of dust, scales and feathers. Its jaundiced eyes were narrow slits in a thin, gaunt frame as it surveyed the revenant and the couple. Its lean lips curled back, revealing small, sharp teeth, as a black tongue writhed in a blood-red mouth and it rasped, "Can't a body get a good night's sleep around here? I'm on the bloody night shift and I need my eight hours!"

It turned and stalked from the room, its wings digging grooves in the floorboards behind it. Muffled oaths and curses accompanied its exit,

"No bloody consideration...need my kip...bloody lovers' bloody tiff..."

The door slammed behind it, leaving an awkward, pregnant silence.

The thing took the opportunity to glance back to the shadows at the gathered horde, huddled against the wall. Wraiths, spirits and demons of different shapes, sizes and varying stages of decomposition glared back balefully. It smiled a ghastly grimace bashfully at them and shrugged a rotted, festering shoulder. Various rancid looks, gangrenous nods and ectoplasmic gestures urged it to try again.

"Umm..."

"What is it?" demanded the man. "My wife and I are using this 'romantic evening' to apparently decide which of us is the worst thing to have happened to the other! What do you want? Spit it out!"

"Eh? Oh, thank you. They get stuck sometimes." The shade spat out a maggot caught between two stumpy teeth. The little white worm wriggled briefly in his filthy hand, before being pushed back into the putrefied mouth and crunched into mush by jagged molars.

"Well?"

"Well, you see..." Despite being drained of almost all blood, it managed to make a very good attempt at blushing. "We have been here for centuries. This house, built by Haitian slaves, erected upon not one but two ancient burial grounds, with money earned through the selling of orphan souls, houses the most foul, diabolical entities known to man. It is built over a gateway to Hell, and its walls reek and ooze with the horror and despair of tortured humanity and eternal damnation–"

"Yes? And?"

The thing blanched visibly.

"It's just that–"

"YES?"

The thing jerked back so quickly that the noise of its rib popping sounded like a gunshot in the darkened room. Shifting its stance slightly to compensate for the jagged bone now poking through the tattered shirt, it continued.

"It's just that we were wondering..."

"Wondering WHAT?"

The creature nervously removed the crusted handkerchief from its breast pocket and gave a good imitation of dabbing away long-dried sweat from long-closed pores on a scarred and flaky forehead. The handkerchief crackled softly as it was stuffed back in the pocket.

"You see, we were put here to show mankind the depths of its own anguish and depravity: a warning, lest it drive itself to insanity and eventual extinction and, well – we were wondering..."

It paused, grinning sheepishly.

"We were wondering – would you like to join us?"

Reflection

Mikayla Hill

"Never look away from your reflection in the Hall of Mirrors." This warning had been drummed into my brain every year when the fair came to town. An old superstition, dating back to when the Fae wandered freely, playing tricks on unsuspecting folk. I was fourteen, old enough to know everything, but young enough that I believed the stories to be true.

The scent of wildflowers floated on the warm summer breeze, our hands were sticky from ice-cream, and our knees scraped from our adventures. Filled with imagined importance, uncaring of the ominous clouds rolling towards the town square, we arrived at the fair with egos fit to burst.

"Truth or dare?"

My turn. As much as I would have liked to pick truth, my pride wouldn't let me take the easy way out. "Dare!" I declared, hands shaking in my pockets.

A cunning glint in grinning eyes was my only hint at what was to come.

"I dare you to spend five minutes in the Hall of Mirrors. Alone."

My grandmother's warning echoed through my mind. Four intense gazes turned to me, daring me to chicken out. None of their grandparents had grown up here; they didn't believe in fairy tales. That disbelief prompting ridicule, only babies were scared of mirrors.

"Too easy," I bluffed with as much confidence as I could muster.

The sign out front, flanked by two funhouse mirrors—one making me tall and thin, and the other short and stout—announced the hall was no funhouse, instead a mirrored maze, designed to disorient and confuse. I decided to only go into the first section, so I could focus on one clear image.

As I entered, I picked a mirror ahead of me, and ignored the infinite kaleidoscope of me's beyond. I locked eyes with my reflection.

"I see you," I whispered to it, voice wavering. "We're just playing a little game, nothing to be afraid of." My reflection didn't look convinced.

Seconds ticked by, ever so slowly. One minute, two minutes, three minutes, four.

BOOM!

The unexpected rumble of thunder shook the walls, and my eyes shot to the exit. Too late, I realised my mistake. I looked back at my reflection; I watched in horror as a malicious smile split its face, too big and no longer mine, it dug now pointed fingers deep into eye sockets. I stared transfixed, as with a silent plop the eyes popped free, speared on pointed fingertips. It waggled them at me, the attached cord of muscle and nerve flopping wetly. Plunged into sudden darkness, I reached up to touch my face. Instead of lashes and eyelids, slick skin met my fingertips, and a scream built in my throat. Sheer terror filled my veins with ice and my throat restricted, squeezing my shriek into a raspy croak. The grotesque image burned into my brain, the last thing I ever saw.

It's not so bad, being blind. At least I don't have to worry about my reflection anymore.

The Tragedy of Montague Bellot

Ryan Fleming

War and pestilence I may have endured with the steadfastness of the saints, but to witness continual desecration of innocents by a man such as this bred a disquiet of faith I could not shake. "How many, o' God? How many lives must be destroyed by Montague Bellot before You will be moved?"

Neither blood from my knuckles pounding the cobble nor my utterance of the Proverbs seemed to elevate my prayers. I should have felt certainty from my lifelong convictions that the sins of Bellot would not go unnoticed by a Holy God who would surely grant the wages of this vile mortal's transgressions. And yet, no such retribution came.

This abominable Montague Bellot, whose atrocities were too oft dismissed as rumors, danced with the devil. No person was beyond the whims of his repugnant pleasures. He strolled, jeweled cane in stride, along the *Notre-Dame de Lorette* or lurked at the crossroads of *Crimee* and *Lorraine*. His preying hands were indiscriminate of the baker, farmer's wife, child poor or noble, for they were his toys – objects of his wrath and damned to sate his lust. When accusation arose, the court found its gaze diverted, by coin or coercion, from the feline smile of Bellot.

As a priest, I seek redemption for all. However, even I could not expel from my fervent prayers the desire for the damnation of Bellot. My prayers went unanswered as neither sword nor plague scourged this depraved creature, and the dam of God's anger was tightly sealed. This heavenly passivity hastened my faith into ruin, and I remained in seething silence within my wooden confessional as the monster prowled freely.

I admit that in my wavering, I dared to wonder if I should have followed my father's trade as a butcher all those years ago rather than as a shepherd of wandering souls. That vocation, at least, would not have required me to wrestle incessantly with the judgments of Almighty God.

But my doubts never precluded me from my duty. A holy man I was and a holy man I would remain. I performed Mass with fervor and furrowed brow. Both the poor and rich received my blessings, and such tender graces were always unbridled. And even when Bellot strutted from his carriage to walk along the *Seine*, flashing the brilliance of his jeweled cane, I bid him a courteous, "Be warm and filled." Yet behind my veiled disdain, a secret confession I dared not speak: the immolation of Bellot burned within my heart.

However, by divine comedy, I found an alliance in a most ungodly individual. Oh, how our dear Savior must have laughed at this union.

In the amber glow of dusk, just before I closed the day's penance, a prostitute, her raiment undeniable, entered my shriving booth. Scarcely had I begun the ritual when she interrupted.

"Father, I come not for blessing. Forgiveness shan't be given if sin be not confessed. I have many sins, and of them, few I would consider repenting." I noted a quiver within her voice. "And yet, I have a bitter inquiry."

"What is your name, child?"

"Lucianna, Father."

"What troubles you, Lucianna?"

Between her sobs, she began, "Father, does God not restrain evil? Why does God not bring justice to those who have been wronged?"

I dared not interrupt her with doctrinal platitudes. "What evil has beset you, my child?"

"I am no saint, Father." Her voice hardened now with anger. "But how can God grant leniency upon one such as Montague Bellot?"

The utterance of this vermin's name cracked my sanctimonious veneer.

The offense was against her sister and brother, her only family. By her carnal trade, Lucianna had provided for them, but the youthful beauty of her sister could not escape the ravenous eyes of Bellot. Her brother, not a day older than ten, fought bravely to defend his sister from the grasp of the demon and was skewered as a bale of hay and cast aside to stain the wildflowers. Bellot's handiwork was unmistakable as Lucianna recounted the violated and broken remains of her younger sister.

"Father, Monsieur Bellot roams free. Free from accusation. Free from consequence. Free from punishment. Must I sit and wait for God to do nothing? In my many sins, might I be absolved of one that brings forth justice?"

My beleaguered spirit feasted on her rage and sorrow. The sun had set, and darkness filled my confessional, blessing me with new clarity – a new purpose. I would no longer sit idly whilst this devil tormented God's children. Nay, if God would do nothing, content to simply listen to my prayers, then I would do what he would not. And I would not be alone in my crusade.

"Lucianna, in Romans, Chapter Nine, God employs all His children to do His will. Some He created to be His objects of mercy and others to be His hand of judgment, the executors of His divine wrath."

I vacated my post and opened the adjoining chamber. The flickering candlelight of the humble abbey hid most of Lucianna's face, yet I found her violet eyes within the darkness.

"Should He call you to act on His righteous retribution, would you accept?"

Stepping out of the confessional into the dim light, she clenched her jaw and bowed her head. "Aye. What is one more unpunished sin? If Hell should be my payment, gladly shall I accept it for the death of Montague Bellot."

I extended my hand to her, saying, "Together then, we shall be the arbiters of God's righteous judgment."

Our companionship must have appeared a delicious scandal, a wrinkled man of the cloth and a woman of the night. But our fleshly desires were to be agents of conviction, and we would only find our satisfaction in wielding God's wrath to smite our villain.

Our allurement would be the vice of Bellot – his lust. His snare would be of his own making. Lucianna was to inflame his desires, and I, the keeper of the Book, would deliver his sentence. As I had with my disturbed faith, I hid all intent of my premeditation from my Order.

Had it not been for our righteous cause, I might have balked at Lucianna's plan, for she possessed a uniqueness of skill that would make any man blush, and tenfold for a man of God. Chains, whips, and shackles adorned her den of iniquity.

My extraordinary ally smiled ruefully upon me. "You would know better than most, Father. Don't all men desire to be ruled, to be dominated by something...or someone? My patrons are the ones who find release in such admittance. Their payment, a tithe to me. Are we so different?"

As it were, our scheme fell on the night of *The Grande Mascarade*. All of Paris was aglow. The masked carnival filled the streets, giving us perfect anonymity, and Bellot's thirst would undoubtedly be at its peak. We had not an ounce of apprehension that we could pick out the stench of his rotting soul from underneath his wooden veil.

Before we embarked into the city, we met in secret within the church, where I dared to beseech a Holy God to deliver this sinner into our ambuscade. Lifting up our final 'amens,' we lowered our carved disguises – the vixen and the fox.

Among the dancers and revelers of celebration, God, seemingly only now hearing my plea, brought the wicked Bellot to us. With brandished jeweled cane in hand, he perused through the music and wine-filled *rues* of Paris, searching to satisfy his hunger, and ignorant of the danger that enclosed him. Lucianna swayed like water, her arms enveloping his person, offering up what could be his next meal. As a guardian angel, I stood meters away with the tool of my earthly father and the Word of my heavenly One, tucked within my robe.

At this late hour, Bellot's intoxication forced him to lean heavily upon his cane, and beneath that demonic mask, the torchlight betrayed his lust-filled eyes yearning for Lucianna. Hooked within our grasp, he seized her, but not before she slithered around to his ear.

I know not her final temptation, no doubt a night of untapped pleasure. As simply as a fly to honey, we trapped our sinner within his vice. As specters, they then slipped betwixt the carnival shadows, and I followed closely behind.

Now within my companion's bowers, as our climax drew near, I prayed that in this delicate moment, no happenstance unforeseen would steal this righteous victory. I, hidden within the room of restraints, watched Lucianna lead Bellot to her altar. Removing his devilish mask, she betrayed him with a kiss, and, undressing him, bade her trembling acolyte follow to her Holy of Holies. His moans of anticipation mirrored my own, yet I kept silent, waiting for the agreed-upon phrase.

"Ah, Monsieur, how wicked you are indeed. Punishment shall be your reward. Yet, am I to be its only distributor?"

Whether Bellot had sensed his impending doom, I shall never know. However, the sheer terror that crossed his face as I, still masked as a fox, leaped from my hiding spot was a delicious *hors d'oeuvre*.

With deft hands, I and my accomplice shackled with chain and rope the credulous Bellot. In his inebriated state, he gave no struggle. We stepped back and admired our naked prey, caught within our tangled web.

He blinked in feeble attempts to comprehend these sudden events. "I say, what is this *injurieux*?" I lifted the wooden mask from my face, revealing the clerical collar at my neck. Again, he squinted, trying to grasp this unnamed horror before him. "A priest?"

"A judge, jury, and executioner. Tonight, Monsieur Bellot, you stand trial for your transgressions," I intoned and withdrew the holy scripture from my robe. "For we shall bring forth God's righteous wrath."

"Enough of this charade, whore. Unchain me at once," said Monsieur Bellot.

Lucianna reached out and stroked the unblemished face of our prey. "Who am I to resist the Will of God?"

"Now, see here," he said as he yanked on his bonds.

With the swiftness of a snake, my hidden blade sliced across his bare flesh. "Bribery!" I yelled. I brought down the knife again. "Malice!"

The parade passed outside of the house, and the cheers of the masked muffled Bellot's shrieks of painful torment. His squeals brought me back to bygone days in my father's butcher's shop. "Lust!" I screamed again, slashing the foul wretch's left eye.

With each committed sin, I produced spurting gashes upon his evil person.

"Adultery!"

"Debauchery!"

"Brutality!"

"Conceit!"

"Fornication!" My cut removed what little manhood he possessed.

I put all my force into a laceration over his stomach. "Murder!"

I pulled back, gasping in ragged breaths. Deep veins of crimson flowed from the writhing Bellot, pooling beneath his chains. After thousands of prayers of 'Thy Will be done' and sleepless nights of vengeful supplication, this egregious sinner's time of judgment had come. Though he was the festering thorn in my belief, I had not been the one whom he had afflicted.

I watched Lucianna revel in the blood splattered across her breast as I handed her the knife. "For your sister and brother," I said with a bow.

Her cold eyes and hands grasped upon my outstretched blade, and with a steady steel tip did she lift the slumped chin of Bellot. His remaining eye fluttered, attempting to focus on his executioners.

"I fear not that Hell shall continue what we have begun," I said with a grin and stepped aside.

"For my sister, Jolie." With both hands, Lucianna drove the blade into Monsieur Bellot's heart, and in one, fluid motion, she withdrew the knife and slid it over the dying man's throat. "And for Jules. Where you are going, neither will you see. *Au revoir*, Montague Bellot."

By the time we unshackled our fiend, dawn was close at hand. Instead of breaking day, darkness gathered above us as we dragged the corpse through the alley's shadows. With what strength remained us, we heaved him onto a manure cart. This sight, the embodiment of my spiritual turmoil, discarded in the excrement of beasts, produced a burst of manic laughter from the depths of my being. Jubilation transformed to convulsive weeping as blackened rain broke from the heavens with the crash of thunder.

Lucianna, to whom I could have granted forgiveness for evil thoughts and never embarked on this journey of vengeance, slowly turned her head to face me. Tears or rain, I could not tell, but a peace rested on her countenance. Lightning ripped through the sky, striking some distance away.

"Bless me, Father. For I have sinned," she said and closed her eyes.

Rain dripped from my robe, washing away the splattered blood. I nodded, and I forced my response, "Give thanks to the Lord, for He is good."

In unison, we whispered, "His mercies endure forever."

Though I had spoken these words a myriad of times, I reflected on this call and response. His mercies...like the mercy God bestowed to Bellot when He ignored our cries for justice? Like the mercy God showed to the ravished victims? No. It was we who chose to deliver mercy to all those now safe from Bellot's malice.

I raised my hands to the violent sky, looking towards the heavens for one final prayer. "God, will You be content to hear the pleas of Your children? Must I continue to enact what You deny? Will You do nothing?"

The response came with a sudden flash of illumination as the lightning found its mark. The glorious light electrified the surroundings, searing all it touched, its thunder drowning out any sound of repentance.

"Merci."

Ten of Swords

Bryn Eliesse

Rolling fog caught the light of street lamps in the velvet night's gloom. Amongst the boisterous crowd of evening goers, a modest table sat nestled within a line of bizarre and flamboyant vendor displays. A black satin cloth adorned the table, complete with a polished mahogany box and a burnished brass collection tin with a curious raven perched on the top.

Clusters of patrons weaved through the thinning crowd, by-passing the humble display, but the man stationed behind the table was persistent. Each night of moderate weather, he sat in the gloom, amidst the chaos and tomfoolery, and simply waited. At last, a pair of females stumbled to his table, smelling of cheap spirits and foolish desires.

"Lovely night to have such beautiful women come upon my table." The flash of a white smile shone beneath the brim of his hat. "My name is Alessio, pleasure to make your acquaintance. May I tempt you with a fortune reading for a mere shilling?"

Alessio opened the mahogany box with a satisfying click to reveal a velvet interior displaying an ebony stack of tarot cards. Running a reverent gloved finger over the top of the deck, Alessio encouraged, "Your past, your present, and, of course... your future. I can ensure that you lovely ladies will not leave this night with a shred of regret." With a sly smile, he asked, "So, what do you say?"

Sloshed giggles contorted the young women's adamant responses, which the man took as a yes. Alessio's raven paced his perch atop the collection tin and watched with a greedy glint in his beady eyes as the women fished for a shilling in their pleated skirts. The raven and its owner only settled when the clink of coin joined the tittering chatter of the women.

With a charming smile fixed firmly in place, Alessio pulled his deck from the box before fanning the cards out before the ladies. "You will pick three and three only from the deck. Simply tap your cards of fate, and we will proceed."

After the women whispered amongst themselves and tapped their chosen cards, Alessio took his time sliding the cards from the deck before arranging each one face down. Setting the remaining deck to the side, Alessio devolved into his spiel of the ways and woes of each of the most basic tarot cards, punctuated with eardrum-shattering squeals of delight.

"I am sure you ladies noticed the dark pallor of my deck. At this hour and in this manner, you may not yet be able to clearly read illustrious and vivid expressions of the cards, but I am an expert at hearing their whispered secrets, never fear." The women, excited by the mystery surrounding the cards and his display, leaned into his space as if they were sharing a great secret amidst a sea of strangers.

Alessio flipped the first card with a flourish; a dark, inscrutable depiction reflected from the slick surface. "Ah, your past, ladies. The Sun with its positivity and great energy in life. You have been assuredly blessed." Bright smiles exchanged between the women confirmed his suspicions, along with the auspicious state of their tailored dresses and neat hair which indicated an affluent past. Perhaps attracted by the young ladies' squeals of delight or the showmanship Alessio possessed, a small crowd of strangers had formed around their table to watch the proceedings.

Alessio revealed the next card with a flourish, showing the same black image. Alessio exclaimed, "Your present! The Four of Wands bringing harmony and celebration." A glittering ring reflected in the dim light, catching the eye of his raven, as one of the swaying women thrust forward a polished hand with a beaming smile, "It's not yet been a fortnight, but I'm engaged!" Again, the fortune rang true amidst the cheering crowd.

"Now, your future." The mass of observers fell silent. Tension was palpable between the ladies who awaited his verdict. Shifting on their feet, the ladies' eyes grew wide as Alessio took his time in caressing the final card with a gloved finger. Just as he turned the last card to yet another indecipherable image, Alessio hesitated, letting the silence linger while the ladies watched with bated breath until he decided to reveal his hand. "The Ten of Cups," Alessio said with a broad grin, "you have long-lasting happiness waiting just around the corner!" Shrieks of delight followed his declaration.

Perched upon the brass container, the raven ruffled his feathers at their shrieks of delight but did not otherwise show signs of life—at least, not until a well-to-do young man singled himself out of the milling crowd. One of the observers in the gathered crowd, the young man, barely of age, with blonde ringlets and frilled cuffs made his opinions known. His boyish voice scoffed, "Idiocy. Though, I'm not quite sure whether the loose cows or the dodgy weasel is more the fool."

The raven's cry pierced the air, where it hung, seemingly suspended in time, startling the inebriated females into momentary stillness with its resounding finality. A stillness encapsulated the group, even as Alessio began to speak.

Pleasure dripping from his voice, Alessio pulled a fourth card from the deck. "How about an encore for your ladies' pleasure? A card for this night and her secrets." Without waiting for a response, Alessio turned the card to reveal the same shadowy image, only this time, he held the image up to the dim light that the street offered.

Alessio admired the crisp lines of illustration on the card, "This is The Ten of Swords. The card, of course, that no one ever wants to see. The man who lies face down with swords embedded deep within his back. He lies shrouded in a vibrant red cape with a dark foreboding sky cast overhead. Powerless. Rock-bottomed. *Victimized,*" Alessio purred.

Beneath the brim of his hat, Alessio's gaze followed the blonde-haired man as he disappeared into the throng. Alessio turned back to the women, a reassuring smile on his face. Into the hush, Alessio said, "I am sure that you beautiful ladies will be perfectly safe this night, as your mistress fortune so ensured with a sacred promise of long-lasting happiness."

Stilted giggles broke the women's silence, bringing the sound of the crowd bleeding into focus once more. The wide brim of the man's top hat hid the pleased glint in his eyes as he promptly wrapped up the reading, declaring a final assurance of health and happiness to the naïve women and a sure promise of a headache to greet them on the morrow.

Alessio stood looming over the two women who scampered off in search of another table to promise them riches and happiness. With calculated efficiency, Alessio arranged the shadowy cards into the polished box. As Alessio tucked the tablecloth and coin collection into an inner pocket of his thick coat, the raven hopped onto his shoulder with sharp, clinging talons.

Stepping forward and disappearing into the crowd, Alessio caught onto the smell of his prey; it snaked along the cobblestone, weaving between the feet of unsuspecting fools.

The darkness grew as the throng thinned. With long, quickening strides, Alessio veered into a dim alley, emerging into a street that was desolate, save for a familiar, homeless face. A greying woman nodded to him before looking in the opposite direction and pointing a single, wrinkled finger towards a dark opening between abandoned buildings. The raven perched upon Alessio's shoulder ruffled its wings before taking flight, disappearing into the night sky with a chilling caw.

With two twists of narrow pathways, the wet road turned to broken patches of urine-soaked cobblestone. A silhouette appeared beneath the jagged outcrop of steel beams that peeked through a dense, industrial fog.

Shining blonde curls reflected in the dead of night, as the distracted young man urinated against a wall. Alessio's shadow grew over the distracted young man. Alessio noted the lusciously conditioned quality as he caught a handful in a tight fist. The boy yelped, hastily trying to secure his trousers while struggling against the towering man. Without hesitating, Alessio turned on a heel and stalked away with his prize in tow. The captured prey put up quite the fight, scratching and yowling like a cornered cat, yet the young man's manicured nails did little to dislodge Alessio's iron fist.

A few streets further into the inner workings of the slums, Alessio dropped his squirming victim onto the broken cobblestone. Wide blue eyes stared up at him with horror. Beautiful, sharp screams echoed off the stone into the ebony night.

A razor emerged from Alessio's high-collared coat, and with a flash of silver, snapped open as he whispered with glee, "Louder." His pleased chuckles harmonized with the younger man's screams until the sounds crescendoed into a grand finale.

Long fingers and a wicked blade, soaked in scarlet, dripped onto the quickly fading corpse. The blonde curls were as unrecognizable as the eyes lying some distance away from their owner.

"One last scream," Alessio encouraged. "Do be sure to make it your best for posterity's sake." With a final slash from his blade, the mangled remnant of a corpse screeched an ungodly howl.

"Perfect," Alessio breathed, letting tendrils of black escape the inner lining of his coat to fill the back alley. In his hands, Alessio held a pristine white card that soaked in the black tendrils, collecting the echoing sound of his prey's final scream.

The young man's twisted face imprinted onto the dark card, almost invisible in the inky black of the background. In a neat print, the card read—The Ten of Swords.

Alessio sighed, observing the card before chuckling fondly, "Always The Ten of Swords."

Alessio could almost still hear the breathtaking reverberations of the young man's final cry as he admired his latest masterpiece. The card hummed with power, vibrating in his grasp, filled with the essence of the last delectable scream. Today's prey was deliciously loud and made a powerful addition to the collection, ready to make his debut the next night, unbeknownst to Alessio's patrons. In the darkness and under the shroud of alcohol-soaked clientele, no one person had ever noticed that each of Alessio's tarot cards were all the very same. The Ten of Swords.

Bringing out the mahogany box, Alessio pulled out the thick deck and fanned the cards to pause and admire his collection of mutilated men. Alessio sealed in the final scream of the young man in his newest card to join the deck, with a definitive click of the silver clasp. He shivered as a rush of power met the adrenaline coursing through his veins. As the clasp closed, the corpse's bloody remains disintegrated into a heavy fog that rose to join the putrid night air.

Alessio fixed his collar and adjusted his hat, tucking away his treasures, just before the gore that soaked his person turned to vapor, shrouding him in mist. The raven returned, landing on his shoulder to squawk its approval.

"Come, my friend," Alessio said as he turned and walked away from the silent alley. "Let us see what else the night has to offer."

Bryn Eliesse

Author's Notes & Bio

"Flesh and Blood" was the first fully fleshed out and finished story I have ever written. It was for a competition based on the theme of 'An Ethical Dilemma', and with this little story, I entered an entirely new realm of writers and storytelling. In this book, you will find an updated edition, but the bones are much the same as the original. This story was inspired by a conversation about a conversation. The questions lingered with me. "What would you do if Jeffrey Dahmer was your son? Would you help him hide the bodies?"

"The Path of Totality" was written for a short story competition, with the theme being a solar eclipse. I turned to research, as I knew very little about them at the time and found quite curious facts... Plants close up and crickets chirp when a solar eclipse arrives. It also follows a path where the moon fully shrouds the sun, called the path of totality. And finally... Umbra–the center and darkest part of a solar eclipse. This turned into Umbar–a giggling child with the darkest of creatures residing within his center... The story flowed from there.

Unlike the other two stories, "Ten of Swords" was written specifically for this short story collection. James Hancock challenged me to create a story inspired by the cover of this book, and I was immediately taken. The shadows and mystery of the man and his raven brought me to a Jack The Ripper, Sweeney Todd-esque side of London.

Beltane, a Gaelic May Day festival, occurring on the days that I wrote this story, solidified the Alessio in my mind's eye, and the cards read themselves.

Bryn Eliesse is an author from the East Coast of the United States. When not drinking tea, you will find her in the literary worlds of romance, fantasy and science fiction. As well as a collection of short stories, she has a half-edited novel, a half-blind cat, and a half-baked idea of what to do with her life. Writing is her passion, so whatever the future holds, it will play an integral part of it.

Christopher Bloodworth

Author's Notes & Bio

In, "A Night Alone," I was challenged to write a thriller that would keep the reader on the edge of his or her seat, and while I don't know if I accomplished that, I did my best to stack tension on tension in a way I hadn't experimented with in any of my previous stories, and I hope readers find the result compelling.

"All the Santas We Cannot See," a sort of light holiday horror story, is the result of my wanting to wrestle with questions of faith and spirituality in a completely non religious story, so of course the myth of Santa Claus was a natural fit. The result is this slightly bizarre, highly philosophical piece that hopefully moves the reader to reflect on the nature of what we can and cannot know as much as it entertains—probably a tall order for a light holiday piece.

Truthfully, I don't know what I can say about "A Family's Honor," a dark comedy/revenge story, other than to apologize that it's so gross—I suppose now is as good a time as any to assure you that all of my stories are non-autobiographical—thank God. I wanted to lean into the absurd and try tapping into that feeling of "oh, I should have said this when they said that!" we often get too late.

And with that, I believe the only thing left to say is to thank you for reading!

Christopher Tully Bloodworth is a serial short story competition participant and honorable mentioner, but he knows deep down his stories are winners no matter what the judges think. He lives in Alabama with his wife (and editor of any of his stories that are worth reading) and two young boys.

James Hancock

Author's Notes & Bio

I have often wondered why I write the stories I write. I think it's because they are the kind of stories I enjoy reading. Troubled characters, a dark path, twists in the tale, and wherever possible, a little grim comedy. Dark comedy nestles nicely in the gloomy world of thriller and horror and can often make shocking situations feel more real.

I've been told my stories often feel like a movie; the reader is a camera moving through the scenes as they unfold. I quite like that. I have a background in screenwriting so that visual element feels normal to me.

With 'Final Trick', I wanted to tap into a gritty urban crime noir story, and have that *realistic* feel. It could happen. It probably has happened. I knew there would be cliché elements, but that was the nature of the beast. Sometimes you simply need a revenge story.

'Vortak: Evil Wizard' came from my love of roleplaying games. What if a portal was opened which went wrong and took the person to an unexpected place? I was in a silly mood at the time and found it humorous having the wizard adapt to our world and be forced to *get a job*. I was fortunate enough to have the story come third in a competition and get published in an anthology book.

'Stretched' is a weird one. I first wrote it as a short screenplay, later adapted it to a prose short story, and then added a little more meat to the bone. As a dark comedy, I'm proud that one piece of feedback I received was it being *too disturbing to give feedback.* I was happy with how the story turned out before, but loved it after that. I guess it falls into *bizarro dark comedy*, and as there aren't many places to give it a home, I thought I'd add it here.

Thank you for reading my stories. I hope you enjoyed them.

James Hancock is a writer/screenwriter of comedy, thriller, horror, sci-fi and twisted fairy tales. A few of his short screenplays have been made into films, his stories read on podcasts, and he has been published in print magazines, online, and in anthology books.

He lives in England, with his wife, two daughters and a bunch of pets he insisted his girls could NOT have.

Jonathan Braunstein

Author's Notes & Bio

The world is full of untold stories; fiction, non-fiction, and somewhere between the two. I desire to create stories with worlds that capture the imagination and touch lives with real, relatable characters. In all, I long to craft stories that linger within a person's soul, encourage, and challenge.

'Mercy and Death' came from my younger days working as a school janitor. It was a thankless, repetitive job, but I loved it. You get to know teachers and students over time, and it feels completely worth it. I liked the idea of a dark spiritual force viewing an elderly, should-be-retired janitor as a worthy foe.

'The Final Confession' is about a juxtaposition of intentions. It is a gruesome expression of situations we can feel trapped by and different ways we can respond. It feels like a story that could be fleshed out for a greater length, perhaps with a known ending.

'The Architect' is historical fiction. It portrays a real life event that happened with horrific historical implications.

I appreciate you reading my stories and hope you find them enjoyable.

Jonathan Braunstein, having worked with college-age students for many years, tends to write lighthearted stories geared toward young adults. On occasion, he writes more twisted tales as found in this collection. He lives in the Midwest USA with his wife, who is also an author. They have two wonderful dogs who don't write much but love everything we write. Currently teaching at a public middle school, Jonathan is also pursuing his master's degree in English and Creative Writing.

Kerr Pelto

Author's Notes & Bio

When you have six grandchildren, you get very creative telling stories at bedtime. There are twists and turns, but the tales I weave are always happy ones.

In writing stories for adults, I can delve deep into my other self and pull out the dark tales, peppered with a pinch of humor.

My sons have a tradition of cozying up with their families for pizza and a movie every Friday night. It's fun. But what if it wasn't? The idea for the noir "Movie Night" was baked from their tradition. Could gruesome movies predict what would happen in real life?

I chuckled as I wrote "Tricks, No Treats." I'm actually a twin. All my life people would ask me, "Are you the evil twin?" I'd say yes, only because I didn't want people to think my twin was. This story delves into the Good Twin vs Bad Twin scenario. But what if both of them are bad?

I have a great fondness for "The Neighborhood." The idea took seed in 2012 after my mother died. For years, she collected little blue and white Delft houses and arranged them lovingly in a row on one of her bookshelves. When I received her ashes, instead of using an urn that had no connection to her, I used one of her Delft houses. Daddy's ashes filled another one. They now dwell side by side on my shelf.

I hope you had as much fun reading my stories as I had writing them. None of them are true. Or are they?

Kerr Pelto is a born-and-raised Southerner from North Carolina. Listen closely; you might hear her accent in her stories. Entering contests feeds her competitive nature and has earned her recognition in publications. A professional calligrapher as well, she has been a contributing writer for the calligraphic world for decades. Don't let her southern, gentile ways fool you. Her stories bely her Catholic upbringing. She might need to go to confession.

Kerr lives with her husband who graciously listens to her ongoing tales. Her house is always abuzz with her grown children, grandchildren, and granddogs, not to mention the chickens.

Mikayla Hill

Author's Notes & Bio

I've always enjoyed writing stories. There is no method to my madness and I like to let the story write itself; I'm a mere conduit for the stories that live within the pocket dimension that is my imagination. A range of things can inspire me, from an old cliché saying to a random thought that flew into my brain. I find that some of the narratives can be dark or twisty. Perfect for this book!

'Nobody Talks to the Grimm Reaper' was my first attempt at something that would intentionally bring a smile or a laugh to the reader. Grimm, a name not a title, was in part inspired by the wonderful character that is Terry Pratchett's 'Death', and the many depictions of Death, or the Grim Reaper, as a robed skeleton. The plot, however, was inspired by a prompt that roughly read "A character talks their way out of death."

'The Monster Within' was my first attempt at a seven-day writing challenge. Random genre and theme assigned day one and deadline for submission exactly seven days later. Now, I may be biased, but it has become one of my favourite short stories I have written, so I hope you enjoyed it too!

'Reflection' is just a piece that I had fun writing. I wanted a bit of a shock factor. After I decided on the opening sentence, the rest wrote itself.

Mikayla Hill is a writer who dabbles in a variety of genres and formats. From poems to short stories, she enjoys the craft of putting words to a page. She started jotting down her weird and wonderful stories when she was eleven; a story where her family dog spoke to her to help solve the mystery of her missing family, and in the end, it was a dream... or was it? She never looked back, and has many notebooks and word documents filled with stories in various stages of completion, from the bizarre and fantastical, to sweet and sappy, to the shockingly twisted.

Mikayla lives in the West Coast wilderness of New Zealand with her partner and two sons, and hopes to one day be able to support them with her writing.

Ryan Fleming

Author's Notes & Bio

    Thank you for taking the time to dive into the strange world that is *Ryan Fleming*. The inspirations for each of these stories are rooted in questions, thoughts, and simple nods to authors who have already made their mark.

    I thoroughly enjoy H.P. Lovecraft's gradual crescendo of fear and terror of the unknown. "The Lost Temple of Osiris" was a piece that I attempted to draw upon that style and form of dread.

    As a Nursing Director for Critical Care, my staff and I are often surrounded by complicated end-of-life situations. Like many family members who are faced with challenging decisions, I frequently wonder *what if* comatose patients could communicate their wishes and the potential horrors that would bring. The reality of such knowledge may not be as freeing as we would wish. I created "M.E.D.I.U.M." to internally wrestle with those family members (and, at times, healthcare professionals) who choose a path for their loved ones that may appear more selfish than dignified.

    My sister and I have very different tastes in music and books. However, we both seem to gravitate toward Edgar Allen Poe's macabre narratives. In the summer of 2022, she and I had several conversations about the dark and twisted stories Poe produced that later laid the groundwork and concept for "The Tragedy of Montague Bellot." I entered the "Writer's Playground One-Year

Anniversary Challenge" with the goal of creating a story that my sister would enjoy. Additionally, I wanted to craft a story that wrestled with an age-old question: "Why does God allow evil people to prosper?" To date, "The Tragedy of Montague Bellot" is my proudest achievement and placed first in the "Writers Playground."

Ryan Fleming is a Director of Critical Care at a hospital in Birmingham, Alabama, USA. He lives with his wife and two children, who are always eager for a bedtime story. Ryan has been published in an anthology and online. With a challenging work schedule, you can find him on many late nights with his laptop, hot tea, and smooth jazz playing as he works on his current work in progress.

Sarah Turner

Author's Notes & Bio

When it comes to dark tales, I love the familiar made unfamiliar; horror rooted in everyday events such as a trip to the local shop where small, seemingly innocuous changes suggest something altogether more unsettling. This is very much the case with 'Human' in which a daily routine exposes the fallout of a sinister event.

With a drive home from work one winter evening, 'A Nice Place to Stay' starts innocently enough before veering into 'Tales of the Unexpected' territory with its mysterious maps and paper towns. New jobs can be tricky; careful out there, folks.

'The Rookery' was gifted, in a sense, by a writing competition. Gothic was the genre; forgiveness the theme. I love gothic tropes—dark omens, rain lashing at the windows, beautiful houses that aren't so much brick and mortar as characters of their own. But as with the other stories, The Rookery is grounded in the everyday—in loss, loneliness, and the home. This is my nod to novels such as 'Rebecca' by Daphne du Maurier, and the rooks are my little tribute to David Copperfield and the nest in his childhood garden.

As someone who isn't loyal to any particular genre, it has been wonderful to dabble in the dark side.

Happy reading!

Sarah loves to write short fiction and poetry, and her work has appeared in publications such as Lucent Dreaming, Writers' Forum, and Writing Magazine. She lives with her partner in England, where she works in education and watches too many quiz shows.

Séimí Mac Aindreasa

Author's Notes & Bio

Inspiration for stories comes from many places. For this collection, I looked towards my love of Horror, War and Comedy for ideas.

A few of my stories have looked at the psychological damage of war, how it can scar and mutilate the brain as well as the body. *Take the Plunge* deals with PTSD, more commonly known as Battle Fatigue at the time of the Vietnam War, when the story is set. How many young men returned from these conflicts with undiagnosed, unseen injuries?

Logs deals with the affect years of carrying out torture and murder has on someone who truly believes themselves to be a good father and husband. Unit 731 was a very real detachment within the Imperial Japanese Army, and the guards did refer to the victims as Logs. I found it hard to believe that each and every guard and soldier at the camps was completely unaffected by what they did and saw.

Proposal is a much gentler subject, in comparison. As well as loving Horror movies, comedy and humour pratfall their way into my stories more often than I intend. I wanted to combine the graphic descriptions of the creatures, with the more realistic arguments of a couple – who probably shouldn't even be together – arguing. Who are the real monsters?

All three stories have some kind of twist to them, which is something I like to put in some, but not all my stories. Hopefully, none of the twists were telegraphed too early.

Séimí Mac Aindreasa, having taken a brief 50-year hiatus from writing, in order to deal with growing up, returned to the field of play with 2023's well received drabble anthology, the Dark of Day, a collaboration between 6 international authors, featuring 66 drabbles. Bring out the Wicked is his second time in print and won't be his last. Raised in West Belfast, he remains there, looked after by Susan and ruled over by their beautiful children and the dog, who Susan is exasperated by. The dog, not the children. Well, also them, sometimes.

If you enjoyed this book of short stories, please look for others on Amazon by the same authors. Thank you.

Bring Out the Wicked

COPYRIGHT © 2023

Printed in Great Britain
by Amazon